Radio Road

Jake Henderson

Radio Road
By Jake Henderson
© 2012

ISBN-13: 978-1479396955
ISBN-10: 1479396958

Cover Layout by Mark Keefer

To my sister, thanks for
many fun Halloweens.

And also to my cousin, Rex,
thanks for all the support...

Table of Contents

1.

The Last Day of Summer

"Wake up, Marshall! Time to get out of bed!"

The shrill sound of his mother's voice jolted Marshall Maddox from his sleep. He closed his eyes, trying to ignore her.

"I'm serious, Marshall, time to get up!"

Marshall rolled over in an effort to escape the sunlight beaming through his window. "How can it be time to get up?" he muttered. "It's the last day of summer."

"Because you need to get used to waking up early!" his mother yelled up the stairs. "You should've been getting up this early for the past two weeks."

Marshall opened his eyes at her response. "And how in the world did she hear me say that?" he whispered.

"Because I'm a teacher! I hear everything!" came the answer from downstairs.

Again, Marshall lay motionless, hoping his mother would give up.

"Marshall!" she hollered, "I'm not telling you again!"

"I seriously doubt that," Marshall mumbled. Realizing the futility of the situation, Marshall threw his covers off and sat up. He stretched and rubbed the sleep from his eyes. Standing up, he crossed the short expanse of his narrow bedroom and peered out the window.

In the distance, he could just see the second floor of his new school. The building looked old and run down, nothing like his old school. The entire structure seemed to broadcast an ominous sense of foreboding. Marshall shivered at the thought of having to attend it.

"It's going to be a long year," he said in a resigned fashion.

He left his room and trudged downstairs to find his mom busily preparing to leave.

"It's about time," she admonished, sweeping by him. "I need to go; I don't want to be late today."

Marshall perked up slightly, realizing what his mother meant. Unlike most kids, he enjoyed the final days of summer break. His mom had to prepare for the coming year, which meant he got to stay home alone.

"Did Dad leave already?" Marshall asked.

"Yep," she answered quickly. "There's cereal on the table if you want some," she suggested as she brushed by him again. "And Marshall, try getting out of the house today. We've lived here for two weeks and you've done nothing but stay inside and mope around."

"That's not true, just yesterday I took the trash to the curb."

His mother rounded on him sharply. "You know what I mean," she snapped. "And don't be smart with me," she added curtly.

"Well, maybe it's because I don't want to be here," Marshall countered.

Mrs. Maddox sighed. "You don't really have a choice in the matter, and it's too late to complain now. Your father and I both got good jobs and we're trying hard to make it work. So please try, won't you?"

Marshall rolled his eyes and smiled weakly. "All right, I'll get out of the house, I promise."

She took a step towards him and kissed him on the forehead. "I know you'll like it here. But I've got to go, so I'll see you this afternoon." With that, she turned and briskly made her way out the door.

Marshall reached up and wiped his brow to ensure she hadn't smeared any lipstick on him. The last thing he needed was to go out in public with giant lips tattooed on his forehead.

He lingered inside for a good portion of the morning. He ate his breakfast in front of the television, something his mother never allowed him to do. Finally, he decided it was time to go up to his room and get dressed for the day.

Even though Marshall had complained, he couldn't imagine staying inside. In fact, he'd had quite enough of this new house. Since moving in, they had been so busy unpacking and putting items in their proper place, that even if he had wanted to leave, there wouldn't have been much opportunity.

A few minutes later, he scampered down the stairs, dressed and ready to go.

"Go where?" he wondered aloud. He had no clue what he should do. For lack of a better idea, he opened the door and wandered outside, surveying the neighborhood for the first time.

It was a miserable, late August day. It was hot, really hot. Heat radiated from the pavement as he stepped off his front porch and onto the sidewalk. No wind and no cloud cover only added to the misery. The heat was one of the first things he had noticed about this new town. The persistent temperature never let up.

He examined his surroundings. There was no sign of movement. All the adults who lived on Radio Road had already gone to work, and all the kids—if there were any—had not yet appeared. He recalled seeing a park down the street the day they had moved in. He decided it might be a decent place to sit and soak up some fresh air for a change.

He walked in the direction of the park and noticed a large, marble slab with engraved lettering that read:

RADIO ROAD MUNICIPAL PARK

The sign appeared rather new and so did the park for that matter. It had a jungle gym, swing sets, a basketball court, a walking track which encircled the entire area, and a vast field perfect for playing football, baseball, or soccer with friends.

"If only I had some friends," he groaned miserably. He ventured to the swings and sat down. He wasn't in the mood for swinging; it just looked like an inviting place to sit.

He had been in the park for nearly thirty minutes, and had just decided to indulge in swinging, when a pleasant voice greeted him from behind.

"Hi, who are you?"

Startled, Marshall whipped his head around, smacking his nose against the swing's chain.

The girl laughed and continued towards him, plopping down in the next swing.

"You surprised me," Marshall explained. "I didn't hear anyone coming up behind me." He watched the girl take a couple of swings. She had straight, dark hair pulled back in a ponytail. Her knees were knobby and showed signs of having been skinned more than once.

"You haven't answered my question yet, who are you?" the girl repeated.

"Oh," Marshall stammered, regaining his whereabouts, "my name's Marshall, Marshall Maddox."

The girl stopped swinging and smiled. "I'm Samantha. Samantha Daniels, but most people just call me Sam." She continued to examine him curiously, almost as if he were an animal at the zoo. "Are you with the family that just moved in?" she inquired.

"Yeah," Marshall replied. "My dad's a psychology professor at the university. He just got hired this summer."

"That's cool," she said offhandedly. "We saw you moving in; I told my brother you looked like a nice kid."

"Thanks," Marshall answered awkwardly. Searching for something else to say, he finally came out with, "So, how long have you been living here?"

Sam thought about the question for a second. "Ever since this new addition was built. I was five when we moved in. All this stuff here," she pointed in the direction of Marshall's house, "even this park was built since then." She turned and gestured in the other direction, towards Marshall's new school, "And all *that* stuff has been there... forever."

"Which house is yours?" Marshall asked.

"That one," Sam said casually, pointing towards the end of the street. "The one on the end."

"You mean the big one?" Marshall questioned.

"Yeah," Sam replied indifferently.

Big didn't even begin to describe it. It was the biggest house on the street, nearly a mansion.

"Your parents must have a lot of money," he suggested.

"I suppose," she responded. She continued eyeing Marshall in a peculiar manner. Finally, she giggled. "Do you know you have lipstick on your forehead?"

Marshall blushed instantly and reached up to where his mother had kissed him. "Dang it, I knew—my mom—I'm gonna—" he muttered as he attempted to wipe it away.

Sam stood up and took a step towards Marshall. "Here, let me help you," she said, smiling. Before Marshall could stop her, she licked her finger and began rubbing the lipstick from his forehead.

"What's going on here?" a taunting voice called from behind.

Sam dropped her hand and turned in the direction of the voice.

"Go away, Baxter. No one wants to talk to you," she said.

"But what if *I* want to talk to *someone*?" Baxter sneered, an expression of mock-concern on his face.

Baxter had thin, black hair, with a bowl haircut and a small, slightly upturned nose. His sharp clothes and clean-cut look reminded Marshall of the kids in his old neighborhood. Two larger, more intimidating individuals flanked Baxter. One was short and fat, while the other was the largest kid Marshall had ever seen.

"Who's this?" Baxter interrogated, pointing at

Marshall.

Sam grinned. "This is my new friend, Marshall Maddox. He's the kid that moved in a couple weeks ago."

Baxter chuckled, "*Friend*, huh? Could've fooled me, the way you two were standing." He started rubbing the forehead of his shorter companion, mimicking the girl's voice, "Oh, let me help you get that stuff off your face." The three boys all laughed uproariously.

This time it was Sam's turn to blush.

Baxter dismissed Sam and turned to Marshall. "So, what school you going to?"

Marshall pointed off behind him. "My mom's a teacher at Goodson Intermediate, so she's making me go there. I wanted to go to the other place; it looks a lot nicer. What's it called?" Marshall questioned, trying to recall the name.

"The Benedict Academy," Baxter filled in. "That's where we go," he gestured to himself and his friends.

"That's right," Marshall acknowledged, "The Benedict Academy. I remember thinking that's a dumb name for a school."

Suddenly, Baxter's demeanor soured. He scowled at Marshall, "What makes you say that?" he demanded.

"Well, you know, Benedict Arnold, he was a traitor to the country, all that stuff," Marshall replied as if this was something everyone should know.

Baxter stepped towards Marshall aggressively. "It's not named after some guy named Benedict Arnold, whoever that is. It's named after my great-grandfather, Harvey Benedict. He was the most respected man in this town and he donated all of the money to have that school built. You should try to remember stuff like that, because my family has a lot of pull around here."

"I'm sorry, I didn't know," Marshall apologized honestly.

Baxter ignored him. "Come on, guys, let's get out of here. Leave the little girl and her boyfriend alone." He stormed off, his large cronies in tow.

"Who was that?" Marshall asked as soon as the three kids were out of earshot.

Sam sighed melodramatically. "That," she explained dispiritedly, "was my older brother, Baxter. He's a jerk," she added.

"I kind of guessed that," Marshall agreed.

"He'll be a 6th grader next year," she informed.

"So am I," Marshall admitted. "Maybe I'm glad I'm not going to Benedict after all."

She laughed. "Well, we're not *all* like that."

"So he's older than you?" Marshall inquired.

"Yeah, by one year. I'll be a 5th grader."

Marshall nodded, pondering the incident for a moment. "Who were those other kids?"

Sam stared at the still departing figures. "The fat one, his name's Ricky, Ricky Russell. He's pretty dumb. The other guy, I can't even remember his real name, everyone just calls him Creature. He's even dumber."

Sam spent the remainder of the afternoon showing Marshall around Radio Road. There wasn't a whole lot to see, just a bunch of houses, a brand new quick stop around the corner, an arcade, and a mechanic shop at the end of the street. As the day progressed, they enjoyed getting to know each other better. By the time they parted, Marshall felt much better, realizing that he at least had one new friend.

2.

The First Day of School

The next day started similar to the one before, with Marshall's mother yelling for him to get out of bed. Today was different, however, and Marshall knew it as he attempted to wake himself up.

"The first day of school," Marshall complained as he crawled out of bed. "Whoever heard of starting the school year on a Friday?" he added. He changed his clothes and went downstairs to join his mother. He found both of his parents in the kitchen. His mom was preparing a sandwich for his lunch, and his father sat at the table reading a newspaper. Marshall flopped down in the chair beside him and poured a bowl of cereal.

"Big day, huh?" his father mumbled from behind the paper. "First day at a new school; are you excited?"

"No," Marshall said glumly. "I want to go back to my old school, at least I had friends there," he lamented.

His dad looked up from the paper and patted him on the shoulder. "Ahh, come on, you'll make new friends."

"I don't want to make new friends. I liked my old ones," Marshall countered.

His father seemed to have decided to drop the issue, but his mother picked it up. "You'll certainly never make any new friends with that attitude," she scolded. "Now, hurry up and finish eating, it's about time for us to leave."

The rest of breakfast passed quietly, and when Marshall finished eating he traipsed back up to his room. He threw pens and pencils, along with his other supplies, into his backpack and raced down the stairs.

Marshall hated having to go to school with his mother. She had to be there thirty minutes before the first bell, which meant Marshall had to be there thirty minutes before the first bell too. Those thirty minutes were the longest and most painful part of the day.

As they backed out of the driveway, Marshall gazed off in the direction of the Benedict Academy. He had toured their facilities with his mother, when they were deciding which school he would attend. The principal boasted about the campus, with all of the computers and other exciting things the school had to offer.

But in the end, Marshall's parents determined that the ultra-modern, private school was too expensive. He would have to attend the Goodson School, which was anything but modern, Marshall thought as his mother pulled into the parking lot.

The campus hosted a mismatched menagerie of four different parts that looked like they didn't belong together. A bronze plaque informed that the main structure dated back to the 1930s. It was an old, redbrick building, essentially a two story cube.

The second portion was newer, but even it appeared thirty or forty years old. A gymnasium stood detached from the other facilities and just behind the gym, a small portable building served as the school's cafeteria. A bronze statue stood out front, in honor of a man named Jim Goodson.

Marshall climbed out of the car and followed his mother into the main building. Fortunately, she allowed him to stay in her classroom until the bell rang, and it was time for him to go to his own class.

Upon entering, his mother instantly began tidying up the room. She had not had much time to organize and there were still several items that appeared out of place. She stopped in front of a life-size skeleton the previous teacher must have used for science lessons.

"Ugh," Mrs. Maddox groaned. "Take this and put it in the closet over there."

Marshall took the skeleton and haphazardly

forced it into the already overflowing closet. "I thought it was kind of cool," he said, shoving the door shut.

She shook her head. "Maybe towards the end of the semester, but I don't want it out here all year long."

The remainder of the thirty minutes passed by and Marshall spent much of the time staring at the clock, dreading the sound of the bell. Finally, it did ring and Marshall picked up his bag, said goodbye to his mother, and joined the growing crowd of students in the hall.

He found his new classroom easily enough. A red, wooden apple mounted next to the door announced his teacher's name, Mrs. Green. She had all of their names on large, paper fish attached to the door. He stared at his fish for a moment before timidly stepping inside.

A woman with long, frizzy, blonde hair looked up with a wide, delighted smile.

"Good morning!" Mrs. Green said in a voice far too cheery. She picked up a clipboard and strode towards him, revealing a pair of jeans and a T-shirt which read '*We Don't Teach, We Inspire!*'. "We're so glad to see you today, tell us your name and we'll find you a place to sit!"

"Marshall Maddox," he mumbled, looking around the empty room and wondering who she meant when she said "we".

"Ahhhhhh," she gasped, bursting into an even

wider smile. "Your mother is one of our new teachers, isn't she?"

Marshall nodded.

"We met her yesterday and she seems like a wonderful person," Mrs. Green continued, glancing at her clipboard. "Okay, let's see, Marshall, Marshall, Marshall, oh—here you are!" She pointed down at the clipboard and picked out the appropriate desk. "Right there. And you can hang your backpack over here on one of these," she said, motioning towards a row of hooks along the wall.

Marshall placed his bag on a hook and sat down. Desks, divided in groups of four, created five islands throughout the room. The teacher's desk occupied one corner, and an additional table, half-circular in shape, filled the other. Posters with clever sayings, a map of the United States, and many items declaring "Welcome Back to School!" adorned the walls.

Mrs. Green set about repeating the same routine of greeting and seating each group of students who entered the room. As they filed in, Marshall observed a broad mix of classmates. Some gave the impression of wealthy or middle-class backgrounds. Others appeared to be from families without much money at all.

Three girls, all with blonde hair, came in giggling and talking excitedly. Mrs. Green directed them to opposite corners of the room, and the girls moaned in complaint as they parted ways. One of the girls sat down across from Marshall, but thoroughly ignored him. Two boys arrived next; they too found themselves on different islands.

A boy in a wheelchair entered and took the desk made to accommodate him. A set of twins came next, and they were split up as well. The kids continued coming, Brenda, Brittany, and Becky, but there were too many names and too many faces for Marshall to remember.

All of the kids seemed familiar with each other and Marshall found himself the focus of many quick glances before his new classmates leapt into conversations about their summers. Another girl entered and sat down alongside the one ignoring Marshall. Obviously pleased with the seating arrangement, the two girls erupted into an animated discussion.

A small, scrawny boy with curly hair and a tall, lanky companion with a buzz cut entered last. Mrs. Green instructed the curly-haired boy to sit across the room, but the one with the buzz cut plopped into the desk beside Marshall just as the bell rang.

"Mornin'," the lanky boy greeted.

"Uhh, goo–good morning," Marshall stammered, surprised at being spoken to.

"My name's Billy Bukes, but nobody calls me Billy. Most folks just call me Boomer," the boy said in a lazy drawl, holding out his hand.

Marshall accepted the handshake. "Hi, my name's Marshall."

"You must be new. I ain't never seen you 'round before," Boomer stated.

"Yeah, we just moved here a couple of weeks ago."

"Well then, I bet you don't know anyone," Boomer surmised. "Let's see, these girls here are Katie and Katy, that's a bit confusin' but you get used to it pretty fast."

The two girls across from them paused long enough to acknowledge that their names had been mentioned before resuming their conversation.

Boomer continued. "That kid over there," he said, pointing towards a boy with floppy blond hair, "his name's Jeremy; he's a great guy. And that fella, the little guy with the curly hair, he's my best friend, John Beavers."

Marshall nodded, trying desperately to absorb it all.

"Then there's the twins, Dave and Mike. I always thought they should have rhymin' names, like all them twins you see on television, but they don't." Boomer paused as if contemplating this dilemma. "And over there is CJ, he's in a wheel-chair," he added suddenly.

"I can see that," Marshall responded.

"He's been in it his whole life, so we've all kind of grown up with him that way." Boomer continued reciting names until Mrs. Green interrupted.

"Hello, class!" she greeted enthusiastically. "This is going to be an exciting year filled with all sorts of things for us to do, and we are so glad we're going to be your teacher!"

Mrs. Green started as most teachers would, by explaining classroom rules and plans for the year. Marshall decided she was likeable, even if she did seem overly excited.

An hour into the day, Mrs. Green's words sent a shiver down Marshall's spine.

"All right, class, since today is our first day, and we can tell that there are a few new faces out there, we want you all to take out a piece of paper and write one page about what you did this summer. Start with your name and anything else you think is interesting, and tell us what you did. We'll give you some time to write, and then we'll let you read them out loud."

"Out loud?" Boomer complained to no one in particular. "I don't care too much for readin' out loud."

Marshall felt likewise, and told Boomer so, but they each pulled out a sheet of paper and began working.

Nearly twenty minutes had passed when Mrs. Green interrupted the silence again. "Okay!" she said brightly. "You all should've had enough time to think of some things you did this summer. Now, we've got all your names in this hat, so we'll just draw them out one at time, and when your name is called, you can share with us what you wrote." She reached her hand into a sleek, back top hat on her desk. "First up, Billy Bukes!"

"Oh no!" Boomer hollered loudly.

"Oh yes!" Mrs. Green responded without missing a beat.

Boomer reluctantly stood up, weaving his way between the desks towards the front of the classroom.

"My name's Boomer," he began, "well, it's not really, but y'all know that," he added, pausing for a moment. "Anyways, I'm Boomer and most of you know I live out in the country, a few miles outside of town. This summer, I spent most of my time hangin' out with my good friend, John Beavers. We spent a lot of time at John's house. I like to hang out in his dad's mechanic shop, that's the Beavers' Mechanic Shop on Radio Road. His dad's the best mechanic in the world. He can fix anything." Boomer stood awkwardly in front of the class for a moment before finishing, "That's all I got, Mrs. Green, can I sit down now?"

"Yes, Billy–I mean, Boomer, you may sit down," she said smiling.

Katy's turn came next. She appeared as nervous as Marshall felt. She spoke of a family trip to Dallas, Texas, where her father attended a dentist convention.

Marshall listened as each student gave a very brief summary of his or her summer vacation. Some had gone fishing, others had worked mowing lawns and delivering newspapers, and others had done nothing at all.

"Up next is Marshall Maddox," Mrs. Green announced.

A slight murmur flowed throughout the room. Marshall heard someone whisper, "Who's that?" as he stepped to the front.

The entire class stared at him with extreme interest.   He was someone different.   He was someone new. He wasn't Boomer or Jeremy or the twins, whom they all knew. He was a stranger.

His hands trembled as he focused on his paper. "Uh–my name's Marshall Maddox, and my family just moved here.   We live on Radio Road," he started in a quivering voice.   However, the words Radio Road seemed to mean something to his classmates.   They exchanged meaningful glances and a couple of girls whispered to each other.

"My dad's the new psychology professor at the university. My mom's a teacher here at this school, 4th grade. She just got hired a few days ago. After my dad got his job, he wanted to celebrate. So we took a family vacation to Australia."

Gasps and oohs filled the room.

Boomer whistled audibly. "Wow, Australia, ain't never been there before!"

Marshall continued. "While we were there, I got to go deep-sea fishing, I went surfing, and we toured the outback where I saw kangaroos and crocodiles."   Again, the class oohed and awed. "Then we moved here and I spent the last two weeks unpacking." Several chuckled at this last part.

"Thank you, Marshall, that was wonderful," Mrs. Green beamed.

Relieved to have survived the ordeal, Marshall retreated to his desk, still shaking slightly. He thankfully returned to anonymity as the few remaining students went forward and stammered through their summers.

Later that afternoon, Katy turned towards Marshall and asked, "Did you say your mom teaches 4th grade?"

"Yeah," Marshall answered, surprised that she had spoken to him.

"My little sister's in her class," she said with a smile. "I hope she enjoys it."

Just then, the small boy with curly hair, John Beavers, burst into the classroom. He had left moments before to use the restroom. He stood, staring wild-eyed at the class before finally managing to spit out two words, "*Ph–Ph–Phantom Pl–Pl–Plopper!*"

Dumbfounded with confusion, Marshall gave Katy a questioning look. Her head dropped to her desk. "Oh no! Not again," she moaned. "That is soooo gross," she added with disgust.

The other students gave similar reactions, but Mrs. Green didn't hesitate. "We'll call for the custodian," she said. She hurried to the intercom and pressed the appropriate button before speaking loudly, "Excuse me, but we need the janitor to come to the boy's restroom on the second floor. He's baaaack," she finished ominously.

"Not again," the voice on the other end complained. "We'll send Eustace right away."

Seeking explanation, Marshall turned to Boomer, "What's the Phantom Plopper?"

"Well," Boomer said, scratching his cheek, "last year, startin' in about February, we'd go into the bathroom every once in a while and there'd be–stuff–all over the place."

"Stuff?" Marshall asked.

"Yeah, you know–stuff. Well, anyways, it was always really gross and the janitor about blew a gasket every time it happened. We hoped it would end this year, but I guess not."

Moments later, an old man lurked through the door. Greasy, gray hair hung to his shoulders and his outfit consisted of a dingy white shirt and stained denim pants.

"That's Eustace, he's the janitor," Boomer whispered.

Eustace raised a hand and pointed a gnarled finger at the class. "I'm watching you brats. I'm warning you, I *will* find out who's doing this. And when I do..." he did not finish the statement, but instead, backed out the door still pointing in an accusatory fashion.

The hours passed with Mrs. Green keeping them

occupied with "first day of school" projects. Marshall sensed that most of the kids wanted to accept him. Several spoke to him throughout the day and others even informed him that they too lived on Radio Road.

Towards the end of the day, Boomer said, "Hey, I've been thinkin' about somethin'."

"What's that, Boomer?"

"Well, me and some of the fellers, we usually hang out every day in John's tree house. It's a whale of a tree house. John's dad built it for us. You'd be more than welcome to join us if you wanted to. It'd give you a great chance to meet the guys," he motioned towards his friends in class, "outside of school, I mean."

Marshall hesitated. Boomer seemed like a friendly enough kid, but he and the others were so very different from the friends he had left behind. "Uhh, I don't know, Boomer, I'm gonna be kind of busy this evening."

"Busy?" Boomer questioned. "What could you possibly be busy with? I know you ain't got no homework," he said smiling, "I'm in the same class!"

Marshall thought quickly, "Oh, well, we've still got loads of stuff to unpack at the house," he lied.

Boomer appeared disappointed. "All right, but if you change your mind, it's right there by the mechanic shop. We're there almost every day—rain or shine."

"Thanks, Boomer, I'll keep that in mind," Marshall replied politely.

Just then, the dismissal bell rang and Marshall swiftly collected his belongings, retrieved his backpack from the hook, and hurried to his mother's classroom.

3.

The Tree House

As Marshall climbed into his mother's car for the ride home, he wasn't in the mood for conversation. He had experienced a busy day and was still trying to absorb everything. His mother, however, never passed on an opportunity to talk.

"So, how was your first day?" she quizzed.

"It was all right," Marshall answered dismissively.

"What's your teacher like? Mrs. Green, right?" she prodded.

"She's okay," Marshall replied. "A little weird, but she's nice."

"Well, that's good. Anything interesting happen?" she continued with her subtle interrogation.

The incident involving the Phantom Plopper

popped into Marshall's mind, but he decided against trying to explain that one to his mother. "Not really," he said eventually.

"Did you meet any new people?" she probed.

He knew this question was inevitable. "Well," he started, choosing his words carefully, "the guy that sits next to me, his name's Boomer, he seemed all right. But I don't know, these kids are just– different."

"Boomer? Oh, I think I met him a few days ago in that mechanic shop on the corner. I asked him what grade he was in and told him that you'd be in his class."

"Yeah, he invited me up to this tree house, but I told him I was going to be busy," Marshall added, but as soon as he said it, he wished he hadn't.

His mother fired a rebuking look his direction. "You know you shouldn't say things like that," she reprimanded. "There's no reason in the world for you not to go. He seemed like a really nice boy. You should be thankful that some of them are already reaching out to you."

Marshall sighed and drooped his head.

"I remember when I was a little girl and we moved to a new town," she continued, "it took months before the kids would even talk to me, much less invite me any place."

"All right, all right, I'll go over there for a little while," Marshall replied, cutting her off before she really got on a roll.

The car pulled into their driveway and Marshall hurried into the house, tossing his bag aside. He wanted to get this over with as soon as possible.

He had just made it onto the sidewalk, when he saw a familiar figure strolling down the street. It was Sam, the girl he had met the day before.

"Hey, Sam," he called.

"Hi, Marshall," she greeted as she approached. "I was just coming to see you," she added warmly. "How was your first day at school?"

Marshall shrugged as he fell in step alongside her. "It was okay, I guess. That school's really run down, though," he said. "Not like that place you go."

"Benedict's not so great," Sam replied. "All they care about is computers. They think computers can teach you anything. Sometimes, I think they care more about their computers than they do us kids."

Marshall thought for a second. "Hmmm, I'm not even sure I saw a computer today."

Sam's eyes widened in disbelief. "Wish I could go there," she said at last.

"I'm not sure you'd fit in over there," he suggested offhandedly.

"What's that supposed to mean?" Sam replied indignantly.

"Well, I just mean–you know, you're–" Marshall struggled for the right words.

"Rich?" Sam offered.

"Exactly."

Sam walked in silence for a moment. "I don't like being rich," she admitted finally. "I wish I was just normal like everyone else," she said. "Where are we going by the way?"

"Some of the kids from school invited me to this tree house. I have no idea what it's like, or what *they're* like for that matter. I just met them today," he said. "I don't really want to go, but my mom is making me. And I'm sure she's probably watching to make sure I actually go," he groaned, slowing to glance over his shoulder. He looked back and scrutinized the mechanic shop at the end of Radio Road. "It's down there," he said, pointing, "behind that shop."

"Sounds like fun, can I come along?"

Marshall shrugged again. "Uhhh, I don't know. I mean, they didn't tell me I couldn't bring someone, but they didn't say I could either."

"Okay, I'll come. The worst they can do is make me leave," Sam decided.

As they covered the ground towards the mechanic shop, the houses became smaller and older. The shop itself sat at the end of the block, next to a rundown home in serious need of repainting. It, and the houses around it, looked nothing like the ones where Marshall and Sam lived.

"So, what do we do, just go into the backyard?" Marshall questioned.

"I'd say so," Sam agreed, leading the way. The Beavers' yard had no back fence, and the moment Marshall and Sam rounded the house, they both stopped and stared, mouths gaped in disbelief. In front of them, nestled in the branches of a mighty oak tree, was the grandest tree house either of them had ever seen.

The structure covered nearly fifteen feet, with sturdy walls, windows and a roof. A porch with railing circled the outer edge, and off to the left, and higher up, a second level connected to the first. A turret, or a crow's nest, topped it off.

"Now *that's* a tree house," Sam uttered in amazement.

"You ain't kiddin'," Marshall admitted.

A set of wooden steps led from the base of the tree up to the tree house. Marshall and Sam climbed the stairs, but realized a full-sized door built into the floor impeded their access.

"What do we do?" Marshall asked.

Sam sighed, reaching up and knocking.

The knob turned and the door lifted, swinging open to reveal Boomer's friendly face. "Well, look who's here!" he shouted. "It's Marshall Maddox, I thought you was gonna be busy?"

"My mom—let me come," Marshall stuttered.

"Who's that you got with ya?" Boomer asked, gazing down at Sam with interest.

"This is Sam," Marshall answered as he stepped into the tree house.

The inside proved even more of a surprise than the outside. A stream of cold air enveloped Marshall, providing instant relief from the sweltering heat. A small air conditioner was perched in a window, opposite an old couch which had definitely seen better days.

The small, curly-haired boy that Marshall recognized as John Beavers sat on top of the couch alongside an Asian boy. They were playing an old videogame system on an even older television. A microwave and a small refrigerator occupied the far corner, next to a table with a couple of chairs and a long bench. Two large area rugs provided the flooring.

"That couch looks really familiar," Sam said softly.

Boomer turned towards her. "It's nice ain't it. We bought that at a garage sale–you know, at that big castle at the end of the street?"

Marshall tried his hardest to stifle a laugh.

"Come over here, let me introduce you to a couple of the guys," Boomer said, motioning towards the couch. "You've already met John, this is his tree house, you know, his dad built it." Boomer smiled and his eyes became a bit dreamy as he added, "That man's amazing, let me tell ya. Anyways," he continued, "this other fella here, his name's Fred."

The Asian boy glanced up, said a quick "Hi," and returned his attention to the game.

"Fred?" Marshall inquired.

"Well, Fred's not his real name," Boomer admitted.   "His real name's Wang-Chung—no, Chung-Kim—no, hold on, I'll get it, I know it's got the word Chung in there somewhere," Boomer stammered.

The Asian boy looked up from his game again and said, "Chung-He Kim, how many times do I have to tell you!"

Boomer seemed relieved that the name had been supplied. "Yeah, well, anyways, that's why we just call him Fred. He's Chinese."

"I'm Korean!" Fred shouted.

"Whatever you say, Fred," Boomer responded. "He's almost as new to the neighborhood as you. Just got here in June. He was adopted by this really nice, old couple that lives next door."

"That's cool," said Sam.

"Let me show you the upstairs," Boomer encouraged.

He guided them up a ladder, leading to an equally spacious second floor with its own unique features.   Stacks of board games filled a bookcase, along with playing cards, checkers, dominoes, a chess set, and even a few books.

"Yep, pretty much anything you could wanna do, we got'chya covered," Boomer offered, correctly interpreting Marshall's expression.

This room had an occupant as well. One of the kids Marshall recognized from school relaxed in a hammock strung up across one corner of the room.

"This here's Jeremy Connors, he's in our class at school, of course," Boomer filled in again, as if reading Marshall's mind.

An unpleasant expression crossed Jeremy's face as he glanced up from a magazine. "Who's that?" he demanded bluntly, glaring at Sam. Before anyone could speak, he answered his own question. "You're that rich girl that lives on the other end of the street. You're *his* little sister aren't you? What's his name, Baxter–Baxter Daniels?"

"Yeah, I'm his sister, but I don't like him!" Sam countered.

"Holy smokes!" Boomer yelled excitedly. "I had no idea! That's almost like havin' the mayor in our tree house."

"Who invited you up here, anyways?" Jeremy asked with a sincere tone of dislike.

"Don't worry about it, Jeremy," Boomer interrupted. "She seems nice enough to me. Hey, let me show you this, it's pretty clever," he said, changing the subject. Boomer stepped over to the wall and unlocked a clasp, releasing a cot with four legs that dropped to the floor beneath it.

"Wow, that's pretty neat," Marshall acknowledged with a grin.

"Yeah, John's dad rigged these up. That way, when we sleep over, we ain't layin' on the floor. Yet, they're out of the way the rest of the time." Boomer folded the cot back up and fastened it to the wall. "Come on, last stop is the crow's nest, up top."

He started up a winding staircase which led to

the turret above. Marshall and Sam followed, emerging on a landing large enough to accommodate three or four people.

The view was immaculate. To the east, Marshall could clearly see the Goodson School; to the west, the park and his own house, as well as Sam's. A portion of the Benedict Academy was visible to the southeast, and a low-lying area of upscale housing additions lay to the north.

"Quite a view, ain't it?" Boomer beamed.

"It's incredible," Sam agreed.

They stood, admiring the view for a few minutes, before Boomer started towards the stairs. "Come on back down, we can get somethin' to drink and visit for a spell."

They followed along to the second floor. Marshall noticed Jeremy had vacated the hammock, and they found him with John and Fred on the first floor. Boomer stepped over to the small refrigerator and pulled out three bottles of pop. He handed one each to Marshall and Sam, keeping the third for himself.

"What do you think of 'er?" Boomer asked, waving a hand at his surroundings.

Marshall looked around admiringly, still soaking it in. "She's beautiful," he responded.

Sam giggled. "Yeah, it's so much better than the tree house my parents bought for Baxter–and they paid a fortune for it."

Jeremy shot a look across the room and opened

his mouth to say something, but Boomer interrupted. "So, what do you fellers think of our new teacher?"

"She seems all right," Marshall offered, before taking a sip of his drink.

"I think she's nuts," Jeremy chimed in.

"John, what do you think?" Boomer asked.

John looked up from the game and raised his eyebrows, as if he wasn't expecting to be spoken to. He opened his mouth, but thought a moment more and finally said, "To be a good teacher, one *has* to be a little nuts. I think she's a *lot* nuts."

Boomer laughed and said, "I think that's John's way of sayin' he likes her." He took a drink and said, "All I know is, if she keeps pullin' my name outta that dang top hat, *I'm* gonna go nuts. Three times today she pulled my name out! Three!"

They all laughed.

"So, how come they call you Boomer?" Marshall inquired, as the thought suddenly occurred to him.

Boomer and John both grinned. "Well, that's a funny story," Boomer began. "Back a few years ago, we were havin' a sleepover in this very tree house. I'd already gone to sleep, but Jeremy and John were still awake. They said I was sleepin' away, and then, just all of a sudden, I yelled *Boom!* in my sleep. Ever since then, they've called me Boomer."

"What were you dreaming about?" Sam asked.

"For the life of me, I can't remember," Boomer said disappointedly. "Must've been somethin' really good, though," he chuckled.

"Probably fireworks again," Jeremy joined in.

"I sure do love fireworks," Boomer agreed.

After a brief silence, Marshall wondered aloud, "What class is Fred in?"

"He's just a 5th grader, but we let him hang out in here anyways, seein' as he lives next door," Boomer explained.

"Hey, I'm in 5th grade too!" Sam said excitedly.

"Small world," Jeremy groaned. "But you go to Benedict! Who'd want to go there? Bunch of stuck-up little–"

"Heck, I'd want to go there!" Boomer interrupted again. "I've heard they've got a computer at every desk, they serve lobster in the cafeteria, and soda pop comes out of the water fountains."

Sam shuffled her feet. "Well, some of that's true," she said meekly.

"A computer at every desk? Really?!" Fred's attention wavered from his game. "Do you get to play videogames?"

The next several minutes passed with a discussion concerning the differences between Goodson and The Benedict Academy before Marshall and Sam finished their drinks and thanked Boomer for his hospitality. It had proven an interesting experience, but Marshall still had reservations regarding his new classmates.

He said goodbye to Sam as they ambled up the cement path towards his new home. Just before stepping inside, he took one last look in the direction of the tree house and smiled.

4.

The Announcement

The first month of the school year sped by in a blur. Between attending class every day and the increased workload of 6th grade, Marshall had little free time at all. He had only spoken to Sam a couple of times and managed to return to the tree house only once. He still didn't quite feel comfortable there, even though the others certainly tried to welcome him.

However, somewhere in the back of his mind, Marshall still believed he and his family would soon be moving back to his old hometown. At the same time, he also remembered how difficult it had been to leave his friends, and didn't want to become attached to new ones, fearing that his family *would* move again.

"Pencils down everyone!" Mrs. Green announced in a singsong voice. "That concludes our standardized testing for the day!"

This school might be new to Marshall, but standardized testing definitely was not. He sat, staring down at the many circles he had filled in, before closing the test booklet and turning towards Boomer.

Boomer tossed his pencil on the desk and flopped back in exhaustion. "Whew!" he said loudly. "That's the hardest test I've ever taken. Askin' me about all them things I learnt last year." He scratched the top of his head through his short, bristly hair. "Why we gotta remember that stuff anyways?" he complained.

"Well, I think–" Marshall began.

"All right, everyone!" Mrs. Green called their attention towards her. She stood near her desk, top hat in hand.

"Oh no!" Boomer whispered. "It's that dang top hat."

"We've got a very special job for..." Mrs. Green said, reaching into the hat, "Boomer!"

"Mrs. Green! That's ten times now!" Boomer shouted in mock indignation.

"Oh, don't worry, Boomer, it's nothing difficult. All you have to do is make a choice for the class," she said mysteriously. "Do we continue on with our next lesson, which will be science, or do we go outside and play kickball?!"

Boomer acted as if faced with a tough decision. "Well, that science lesson sounds mighty temptin', Mrs. Green, but I'm gonna have to go with kickball!" he answered.

"Kickball it is!" Mrs. Green agreed.

Once on the playground, Mrs. Green utilized the top hat to sort teams, so no one would feel left out or teased due to lack of athletic ability. CJ volunteered to be the pitcher for both sides.

Marshall, Boomer, and John ended up together, but Jeremy found himself on the opposing team. Marshall took his position in the outfield and watched as several kickers took their turn. Two got out and one reached base. Jeremy kicked fourth and booted the ball hard in Marshall's direction, and it appeared to be sailing far out of reach. Marshall spun around and hustled backwards, trying to close the distance. He stretched and made a spectacular one-handed catch. Everyone oohed and awed, impressed by the unexpected display of athleticism.

With the third out recorded, Marshall and his teammates jogged to the infield, passing Jeremy along the way.

"Nice kick," Marshall said politely.

Jeremy merely glared back in frustration.

The first kicker on Marshall's squad, David, reached base safely. His twin brother, Mike, also succeeded, placing runners on first and second. Katy's kick sailed straight back to CJ, who made a great catch, recording their first out. Next, Boomer kicked the ball solidly, but Jeremy made an excellent grab in the outfield.

Marshall's palms began sweating as his turn approached. No one at this school had seen him compete in any kind of athletic activity, so he hoped to do his best. He assumed his position at home plate and waited. He allowed the first pitch to pass by, desiring a better one. The second also proved unsatisfactory. A few students began yelling things such as "Ahh, come on, just kick it already," or "That was a good one, what're you waiting for?"

The third roll was perfect, and Marshall kicked the ball with all his might, sending it soaring over the infield. Jeremy raced back just as Marshall had done earlier, in an attempt to field the ball, but it bounced safely over Jeremy's outstretched hand and rolled towards the fence. Marshall rounded third base as Jeremy retrieved the ball and threw it towards the infield. Marshall touched home just before the catcher recovered the ball. His teammates cheered and congratulated him with high-fives.

The game continued with Marshall scoring several more runs for his team. Jeremy's team played rather well too. Although, partially due to the fact that John Beavers abandoned his post in right field to visit the restroom. Jeremy's squad capitalized and scored several runs in his absence. Twenty minutes later, they were thoroughly unwound from their testing experience.

"Okay, everyone!" Mrs. Green shouted. "Time to go back in, we can't stay out here all day!"

Some protested vaguely and a few muttered, "Can't we play just a little longer?" but most reluctantly lined up without argument.

"Well, that was a great game," Boomer declared to anyone who would listen. "You can really kick," he added, turning to Marshall.

"Thanks," Marshall said, smiling faintly.

As they entered the building, Mrs. Green allowed them to stop for a restroom break. "Three at a time, three at a time," she announced as they lined up.

Jeremy, Boomer, and Marshall all stepped through the door together. They had just entered when they stopped and stared at the floor in appalled disbelief.

All three spun on their heels and burst back into the hallway.

"Phantom Plopper!" Boomer hollered, causing both 4th grade classes across the hall to look up from their desks.

"Oh, that is soooo gross," Katy moaned from a few feet away.

"Did you see that stuff?" Jeremy gasped.

"Don't remind me," Marshall replied, trying to flush the image from his mind.

"We'll call Eustace," Mrs. Green announced calmly.

"No need," yelled a gravelly voice.

Marshall and the others whipped around to find Eustace the Janitor emerging from a closet just to the right of the girl's restroom.

Eustace pointed at Boomer. "I could have heard this one bellowing a mile away."

"What was he doing in the closet?" Jeremy whispered.

Marshall snorted with laughter.

Eustace turned his attention away from Boomer, singling out Jeremy and Marshall. "I'm warning you, little punks–" he started, but again, stopped short of finishing his threat. He wheeled his mop bucket into the bathroom, muttering something about kids having no respect for their elders.

A moment of awkward silence ensued before Mrs. Green interrupted. "That was exciting," she said happily. "For those of you who didn't get to use the restroom, we can use the one upstairs."

Several minutes later, they settled into their desks.

"Okay, class, we've had some fun, but now it's time to get out those science books. We have a really wonderful lesson for you today!"

"Ahhh, man," Boomer complained, pulling his book out from under his desk. "I thought we was gonna get out of this–"

But the intercom interrupted. "May I have your attention," came the voice of the principal, Ms. Johnson. The sound resonated throughout the entire school, echoing from every speaker in the building. "We're going to have a surprise assembly today. Could all teachers please lead your classes to the auditorium at this time," she concluded as the intercom fell silent.

"Where's the auditorium?" Marshall wondered aloud.

"Oh, that's just the gym. It's also our auditorium. Sometimes they call it the multi-purpose room. And sometimes they call it the Gym-atorium. It's a little confusing, but it's all the same place," Boomer explained.

Mrs. Green seemed uncharacteristically disgruntled. "Okay, we weren't planning on an assembly, so there'll be no science lesson today," she apologized. "Everyone line up, and we'll head down to the gym."

As they marched towards the gymnasium, they speculated about the assembly. "What do you think this is all about?" Boomer asked to no one in particular.

"I have no idea," Jeremy answered.

"Maybe they'll have a fireworks display. That'd be neat, wouldn't it?" Boomer suggested.

"I doubt it Boomer, not inside," Marshall commented.

"How about one of them strong-man shows," Boomer guessed again. "My cousin was tellin' me that these fellers came to his school once, and they was doin' all sorts of stuff. Rippin' phonebooks in half, bending bars with their teeth, and breakin' cement blocks with their head."

"Could be, but I doubt it," Jeremy said.

Students sat on the gym floor according to age, putting Mrs. Green's class of 6th graders at the very back. Jeremy plopped down first, with John and Boomer following close behind. Marshall took a seat alongside Boomer and they waited for the remaining students to file in.

Finally, Ms. Johnson took the stage. Marshall had only seen her twice before, the day he had enrolled, and once when she had come into the class to speak to Mrs. Green. She was a short woman with long, dirty-blonde hair. She was professionally dressed, and carried herself with a confident demeanor.

"Welcome to our assembly today," she greeted, speaking with a slight drawl. "Sorry this was such short notice, teachers, but when the Chamber of Commerce comes calling, you have to accept," she apologized. "Okay, we have very exciting news for the school, and the head of our local Chamber of Commerce, Mr. John Daniels, has asked if he can make the announcement. So, without further delay, here he is, Mr. John Daniels!"

A smattering of applause greeted the visitor as he approached the microphone. Boomer leaned over to Marshall and whispered, "I think that's your friend Sam's dad."

Mr. Daniels' tall frame hunched over to speak into Ms. Johnson's microphone. "Thank you, guys, for letting me visit with you, I'm sure you're terribly disappointed you're not in class right now," he paused, as if expecting laughter that never surfaced. "I just came here today, because I wanted to announce a really exciting event that will be occurring just a little more than a month from now."

Marshall glanced down the row and gave Jeremy a questioning look. "A month from now?" he asked quietly.

Jeremy shrugged and mouthed the words, "I don't know."

Mr. Daniels continued, "You see, every year, each school has its own carnival. Here at Goodson, you always have one in the spring. Over at my son's school, Benedict, they always have theirs in October."

A chorus of boos accompanied the mention of Goodson's rival school.

The booing flustered Mr. Daniels for a moment. "Yes, well, it's nice to see the old rivalries are still going strong," he joked. "However, we've been talking to the area schools for quite some time now, and we've decided that instead of a whole bunch of small carnivals, that we'd rather have one, big, town-wide carnival on Halloween night!" he announced dramatically.

A murmur of excitement swept through the auditorium.

"A carnival on Halloween night!" Boomer said

loudly. "That sounds like it ought to be a blast!"

"But that's not all," Mr. Daniels announced, quieting the audience again. "There's going to be a contest between all the classes who have a booth at the carnival."

"Contest?" Boomer repeated.

"Whichever class raises the most money at their booth, the Chamber of Commerce will reward that group with a trip to Wonderland, with the winner being announced the night of the carnival!"

An even larger roar of excitement rippled across the auditorium.

"What's Wonderland?" Marshall inquired.

"It's an amusement park about a hundred miles from here. I've only been there once, when I was a little kid, but it's a heck of a lot of fun," Boomer filled in.

Marshall heard several other similar comments. "I've never been there," one student whispered. "I'm always asking my dad to take us, but he says it's too expensive," another admitted. A third replied, "I always see it when we drive by, but I never even ask because my mom can't afford it."

Mr. Daniels allowed the buzz of the crowd to subside before continuing. "There's one thing I almost forgot to tell you," he said, still stooping over the microphone. "The Chamber also decided to have this new annual carnival, just over here," he pointed in the general direction of Marshall's house, "in the brand new Radio Road Municipal

Park."

Many students, including Marshall, cheered this announcement.

"Hey, that'll be somethin'. A great big ol' carnival right there on Radio Road!" Boomer shouted.

Mr. Daniels continued, "I know Radio Road is special to me and a lot of others around here. Why, I can even remember back when I was a kid, all that was out there was an old radio station. It sure has come a long way since then. I'm sure all of you are aware of the renovations that have taken place and we thought this carnival would be a great chance to show off everything that's happening, especially the new park."

Several of the teachers clapped.

"So, thanks for having me and as Halloween draws near, Ms. Johnson will fill you in on the details. Thanks again." Mr. Daniels waved and stepped off the stage, carelessly bumping the microphone and causing it to emit a shrill sound. The noise seemed to wake the students from a daydream and a sudden buzz of a hundred voices instantly permeated the atmosphere.

The rest of the afternoon was filled with talk about Wonderland and the Halloween Carnival. But most didn't seem nearly as excited as Marshall believed they should be.

Before the bell rang, he asked Boomer, "So, how come no one seems that excited about the carnival and Wonderland?"

Boomer pondered the question for a moment. "Hmmm, probably 'cause of them Benedict kids. Some of them kids have been hasslin' us our entire lives.   We were all mixed together in elementary school.   Why, I myself went to 1st Grade with Baxter Daniels. It was no fun, let me tell ya."

"But what does that have to do with anything?" Marshall questioned.

Boomer didn't have time to answer.   Jeremy leaned over and interrupted. "Think about it. Who made that announcement? Mr. *Daniels*. You heard him, his son goes to Benedict. We haven't got a chance at beating them."

Boomer nodded. "You can say that again. Them Benedict kids would sure be one tough nut to crack."

5.

The Game

The next week passed by smoothly. The initial buzz surrounding the carnival died down, and Marshall had not heard anyone make reference to it in several days. It seemed that most of his classmates agreed with Jeremy and Boomer. The Benedict kids just couldn't be beat.

It was the end of the first week of October before Mrs. Green mentioned it to the class again.

"Okay, kids," she said brightly at the end of school on Friday. "It's officially October now, which means the Halloween carnival is only a few weeks away."

A general murmur crept through the room, halfway between excitement and a groan.

"This weekend, we want you all to think about

possible ideas for our booth. We're sure you all want to win that big prize, so think really hard, and come back to us next Monday with some great ideas!"

"Great ideas?" Boomer repeated in disbelief. "I ain't had one of them since this past summer."

Jeremy rolled his eyes. "Yeah, and that one got you grounded for six weeks."

All afternoon, Marshall racked his brain, trying to come up with some brilliant idea that would help his class win the carnival. He had a few good ones, but none of them seemed big enough, either that, or he knew other classes would already be doing the same thing. He tossed and turned for several hours in bed that night, mulling over the problem in his head.

The following morning presented a beautiful fall day; brilliant shades of orange, yellow, and red filled the trees. A deep-blue sky stood overhead. The air was crisp, but not cold. The sweltering heat from August and early September had finally fizzled and once again, it felt good to be outside.

Marshall decided to walk to the end of the street and visit Sam, since it had been over a week since he had seen her. He hopped down the steps of his porch and ambled his way towards her home.

Several minutes later, he stared up at the impressive structure. It was, without a doubt, the largest house on Radio Road. It stood two stories tall but seemed to tower over the neighborhood.

The morning sunlight reflected off the structure's vast number of windows. Marshall marveled at the tall, high-reaching, white columns in front. Up above, the steep slopes of the peaked roof stretched skyward. A wrought-iron fence enclosed the remaining three-fourths of the property. The entire estate seemed intimidating, yet strangely inviting at the same time.

Marshall timidly stepped onto the porch. As he reached for the doorbell, the door burst open. He found himself face to face with Baxter Daniels and his two cronies, Creature and Ricky.

"What are you doing out here?" Baxter asked rudely, not caring for an answer. "Out selling trinkets door-to-door? Raising money for that pathetic little school of yours?" he harassed. "Creature used to go there, didn't you, Creature?" Baxter said, slapping his enormously large friend on the shoulder.

The giant responded with a grunt.

"What was it you said their cafeteria smelled like, Creature?" Baxter prompted.

Creature laughed moronically. "Smelled like they were cooking dog food," he replied.

Baxter and Ricky both hooted with laughter.

"Hey, maybe that's it," Baxter snorted. "He's collecting canned goods for the school cafeteria." He turned back into the house and hollered, "Hey, Sis, your boyfriend's standing on the porch!"

"She's not my girlfriend," Marshall muttered.

"Whatever you say, Mitchell," Baxter said, stepping off the porch.

"Marshall," Marshall corrected.

"Whatever. Come on, let's get out of here, guys," Baxter ordered as he and the two others turned their backs and walked away.

Marshall stared at them, wondering how someone could possibly be so rude. A hand sud-denly grabbed his elbow. He spun around, startled, to discover Sam still wearing her pajamas.

"Are you gonna stand on the porch all day?" Sam questioned.

"Oh, sorry," Marshall began. "I didn't realize you weren't out of bed yet."

"Well, I'm standing here aren't I?" Sam giggled. "So, I'm obviously out of bed."

"Come on in while I go upstairs and change," she offered.

"Uh–okay," Marshall awkwardly agreed.

Stepping into the home felt like walking into a museum, or one of those fancy stores where it seems that everything might break. The interior of the house was even more pristine than the outside made it appear. From where Marshall stood, he could see a formal dining room with a crystal chandelier and a cabinet filled with delicate champagne glasses.

In the opposite direction, a lounge featured fragile-looking antique furniture, which did not appear as if it were intended to be sat on. Sam led him into a third room, which served as a living room, or a den. This area didn't look too terribly different from Marshall's own home. A television filled one corner and the sofa in *this* room showed signs of day-to-day use.

"I'll be down in a minute," Sam said, disappearing up a flight of stairs.

After Sam vanished from sight, something in the corner caught Marshall's attention. A man sat back in a recliner with a newspaper stretched out in front of him. Unable to see the figure's face, Marshall assumed it was Sam's father, who had spoken at Goodson. A small, fluffy, white dog sat in the chair with him, staring curiously at the newcomer.

Marshall attempted to sit down as quietly as possible, hoping Mr. Daniels might not even notice him. But no sooner had he sat down, than the small dog yapped loudly. Mr. Daniels folded the newspaper and studied Marshall with a friendly face.

"Hello there," Mr. Daniels said. "And who might you be?"

Marshall's voice caught in his throat momentarily. "My–my name's Mar–Marshall," he croaked. He suddenly felt a desperate need for something to drink. "I'm a friend of Sam's."

"Oh, you're the boy Sam's been telling us about. Your father is a professor at the university, right? Dr. Maddox?"

Marshall nodded in acknowledgment.

"Yes, I met him not long ago. Seemed like a really nice man." Mr. Daniels shuffled his newspaper and dropped it to the floor beside him. "So," he continued, "Sam tells me you go to Goodson, is that right?"

"Yes, sir," Marshall responded.

Mr. Daniels nodded approvingly. "That's a good school. Little worn around the edges these days, but they do a real good job there." He sat up a little straighter and leaned towards Marshall. "You know, my mother went to Goodson. But that was a long time ago, before they built Benedict, of course."

Just then, Sam came bouncing down the stairs in a pair of jeans and a T-shirt, her hair pulled back in its usual ponytail. "Ready?" she inquired.

Marshall nearly jumped from his seat. "Definitely," he said, in what he hoped sounded like a casual tone.

"You kids have fun," Mr. Daniels encouraged as they slipped out the front door.

Once back outside, Marshall breathed properly for the first time in minutes.

Sam giggled. "What's the matter?" she asked.

Marshall gestured over his shoulder. "I just wasn't expecting your dad to be there, that's all," he said honestly.

"You came to my house on a Saturday morning," Sam said, still laughing under her breath. "Where'd you expect him to be?"

Marshall shrugged, "Off doing Chamber of Commerce stuff?" he guessed weakly.

"Yeah, he's been doing a lot of that lately," she admitted.

"He came to our school a couple of weeks ago, did he come to yours too?" he asked.

Sam snorted. "What? Do you think he'd actually miss an opportunity to come to the *great and glorious Benedict Academy,*" she said dramatically. "The historic school his wife's grandfather built. The school where his *only son* goes. You should've heard him up there, going on about how proud he was that his son goes to *Benedict,*" she said with obvious frustration.

"What about you?" Marshall asked.

Sam laughed again. "Never mentioned me once," she said flatly.

Marshall suddenly felt the need to divert the conversation. "So, what do you think about this Halloween carnival?"

"It sounds pretty cool, I guess," Sam said. "But we have a Halloween carnival every year at Benedict. The only difference is this one will be bigger and in a different place."

"What about the contest?" Marshall inquired.

"My brother and his friends are convinced that they're going to win. And he's probably right, my parents and all the other parents will basically buy off the whole thing for them."

"Yeah," Marshall agreed, "that's how most of the

kids in my class feel. Some of them act like they don't even want to try."

"Hmmm," Sam said, furrowing her brow. "They shouldn't be so sure–"

Sam got no further with her thought. They had just come into the clearing that revealed the park, and Marshall instantly saw what was bothering her.

They were still a good distance away, but Marshall could clearly make out the figures of Baxter, Creature, and Ricky playing catch with a red ball. A small boy with extremely curly hair struggled in vain to recover the ball, as another dark-haired boy pushed himself up off the ground.

"Isn't that your friend, John Beavers?" Sam asked. "And that other boy is Fred, isn't it? The Korean boy?"

Marshall sighed. "It sure looks like it."

Sam's hands shook and her voice trembled. "My brother and his thugs," she said, storming towards them. "Someday, they're going to run into someone who's tougher than they are."

Marshall reluctantly followed. He had no desire to pick a fight with Baxter Daniels and two of the largest 6th graders he had ever seen, but he also knew that he couldn't just sit by and watch them victimize John and Fred.

"Hello, Sis," Baxter said casually, apparently unaware of just how angry Sam was.

"Give it back!" Sam shouted.

Baxter laughed defiantly. "Oh yeah? And who's

gonna make me, you or Maurice there?" He held out the ball towards Sam. She lunged for it, but he pulled it back just in time. "Ooh, too slow, Sam, want to try again?" he admonished, presenting the ball once more. Again she swiped at it, and again he pulled it away.

"Baxter!" she yelled. "You are such a—"

"Such a what?" Baxter challenged. "Better watch what you say, little sis, or I'll tell *mommy*," he pronounced the last word sarcastically. He took the ball and bounced it off John's forehead. John's reflexes were too slow and it rebounded into Baxter's hands before John could even move.

"Hey, Creature! Catch!" Baxter shouted.

Just then, Marshall reacted. He had seen and heard enough. He ran in front of Creature, sprang up and caught the rubber sphere. He landed in a crouch and felt Creature's mammoth arms swipe the air just above his head.

"Nice catch, Martin," Baxter sneered.

"Way to go, Marshall!" Sam shouted sincerely.

Marshall barely had time to react. Both Ricky and Creature tried to tackle him instantly. He slipped through both of them and tossed the ball to Sam.

"Give that back!" Baxter yelled, chasing after his sister.

Sam threw it to John, who immediately slung the ball high in the air as soon as he saw Creature charging towards him.

Creature caught the ball and threw it towards Ricky. Ricky stretched but Marshall made it there first.

"I'll get you for that!" Ricky panted.

"Hey, throw it over here!" yelled a new voice. Marshall looked and realized that Boomer had appeared out of nowhere.

Just then, Baxter blind-sided Marshall and took him to the ground. "Don't play with the big boys unless you want to get hurt," Baxter said coolly, resting on top of Marshall.

The ball had rolled free, however, and Fred picked it up. Surprisingly fast and agile, he evaded Ricky, who was out of breath. Unfortunately, he ran straight into the arms of Creature, who easily ripped the ball away.

Creature tossed it to Baxter, who had returned to his feet. But just as Baxter prepared to heave it to Ricky, Sam swiped the ball from behind and squeezed it tight. As mean and tough as Creature and Ricky were, not even they were willing to tackle a girl.

For a moment, Baxter seemed to consider his options, but he finally turned away. "Fine, keep your stupid ball," he muttered. "Come on, guys, let's get out of here and let the babies play with their toy."

As they stormed off, Creature shot a hateful look at Marshall; Ricky, on the other hand, was too out of shape to do anything but pant heavily.

Baxter whispered, "Looks like your girlfriend saved the day."

"She's not my girlfriend," Marshall said quietly to himself.

Once they were at a safe distance, Sam finally relinquished her death grip on the ball and handed it gently back to John. "I think this is yours," she said with a smile.

John accepted it and said, "Thanks." He looked down and added, "Ain't no one ever stood up for me before, 'cept my dad."

Marshall smiled, not sure how to respond.

Sam laughed. "Well, you shouldn't worry too much about my brother. He picks on everyone, including me. He's just a no good punk."

Boomer patted John on the back. "You got that right," he said in agreement. "Why, he'd pick on a three-toed skunk at a rat-shootin' festival."

"Huh?" Sam asked, confused.

Boomer continued. "Now, why don't you two come on down to the tree house with us and have a drink," he offered, motioning toward the end of the street. "You've earned it."

6.

The Big Idea

The five of them quickly walked the short distance from the park to John's. They rounded the house and climbed the steps of the tree house, opening the door to find Jeremy waiting for them. He was lying on the sofa, and appeared to be in a sour mood.

Jeremy sat up and scowled as they lumbered inside. "Off having fun without me?" he asked irritably.

"Well, heck no," Boomer said. "In fact, we sure could've used your help." He pulled out one of the chairs next to the table and flopped into it. "It was Baxter and his buddies!"

Fred raised his arms in protest. "Yeah! Those no good–" Fred said something in Korean which Marshall couldn't understand, but was sure none of their parents would approve of. "They've always got to ruin everything," Fred finished in English.

All five of them immediately launched into a thorough account of the keep away game with Baxter. Fred and Boomer talked animatedly while Marshall described the moment Baxter tackled him. John laughed and nodded as they divulged the story. By the end, Jeremy looked like he had definitely heard enough.

"Boy," he sighed, "sounds like you really *were* having fun without me."

"You should've seen Marshall, though," Boomer pressed on. "He was somethin' else."

Marshall smiled, but tried to shrug off the compliment. "It was nothing, really," he mumbled.

Sam slapped him playfully on the arm. "No, it wasn't *nothing*," she argued. "Baxter needs to lose every once in a while, he's always won—at everything."

"Hey, speakin' of Baxter, that reminds me of somethin'," Boomer interrupted. "Have any of you ever seen that mannequin at the Save-Mart? It looks exactly like Baxter!"

John began shaking with silent laughter.

"What?" Jeremy asked, puzzled.

"In the boys' clothin' department, there's this dummy that they've got all dressed up. It has the exact same haircut, even the face is a spittin' image."

Sam began giggling. "I think I know which one you're talking about. That's hilarious, I've always told him he was a dummy," she said through her laughter.

"Wow, I'm surprised a girl like you has ever even been to the Save-Mart," Jeremy scoffed.

Sam rolled her eyes. "We go there for all sorts of things. Just the other day, my mom bought some new Halloween decorations."

"Speaking of Halloween," Marshall began, seeing an opportunity to broach the subject of the carnival. "Have any of you guys been thinking about the carnival?" He could instantly tell by their expressions that they didn't *want* to think about the carnival. "Mrs. Green told us to come up with some good ideas by Monday. I thought about it last night while I was trying to sleep."

"Well, let's see," Boomer started. "Last year, we had a booth where people threw darts at balloons. That was pretty fun."

"And the year before, we did a duck pond for little kids," Jeremy added. "Where they could win prizes by *fishing* over a wall," he explained. "That *wasn't* fun."

"My cousin said his class is doin' a cakewalk, and his mom's gonna make a bunch of cakes. I'll tell you what, that woman makes the best cakes ever," Boomer informed, rubbing his stomach in appreciation. "And there's another class that's got a deal worked out to play some sort of bingo game with a cow. I don't exactly know how a cow's gonna play Bingo, but it sure sounds interestin'."

Marshall considered those ideas for a moment. "What's your class doing?" he asked Sam.

"My class has decided on a dunk tank, that's what the 5th grade usually does at our carnival," she answered.

Boomer whistled in amazement. "That sounds pretty sweet, where you gettin' the dunk tank?"

Sam shrugged. "I think someone's dad is having it built for us."

Boomer slapped his thigh. "Gee, wish we'd have thought of that. John's dad could've built us a whale of a dunk tank."

"But see," Jeremy cut him off, motioning towards Sam. "This is what bugs me the most. It's not *our* carnival, it's *their* carnival."

"Whose carnival?" Boomer responded, slow to understand.

"The Benedict Academy," Jeremy clarified. "They're the ones who always have the carnival in October. All the best booths will be theirs, all the best prizes will be theirs," he stopped for a moment in frustration. "It feels like they're just using this as an excuse to embarrass us."

"Well, I don't know about all that," Boomer said, scratching his head, "but a Halloween carnival sure sounds like a fun time to me."

Fred looked confused as well. "Uhh, I've been wondering something, guys," he finally asked.

"What *is* Halloween?"

They turned and stared in disbelief.

"You don't know what Halloween is?" Jeremy inquired.

"What?" Fred snapped in agitation. "I just moved to this country three months ago. Half the time I don't have a clue what you guys are talking about."

"You mean to tell me they don't have Halloween in China?" Boomer asked, astonished.

"I'm Korean!" Fred shouted. "And no, we don't have Halloween in Korea. They probably don't have it in China either, but I don't know because I'm not Chinese!"

"Man, can you imagine," Boomer gasped, "a feller not even knowin' what Halloween is?"

"Would someone please tell me what Halloween is?" Fred pleaded in exasperation.

"Halloween is a holiday," Marshall told him.

"It's a really cool holiday!" Boomer picked up the explanation. "Where kids dress up in costumes and go door-to-door, asking people for candy."

For a moment, Fred looked amazed. "You mean, you just walk up to complete strangers' houses and say, 'give me some candy!'?"

"No, you're supposed to say, 'trick-or-treat'," Jeremy offered.

"Trick-or-treat?" Fred questioned.

"Well, if they don't give you any candy, then you're supposed to play some sort of trick on them,"

Sam informed.

Fred still looked confused. "Then why isn't it 'treat-or-trick'?"

They all sat and thought for a second.

"Don't ask such difficult questions," Boomer retorted, breaking the silence. "The point is, when you go trick-or-treatin', you get tons of candy. And sometimes it's better than candy—popcorn balls, caramel apples, candy apples—it's some good stuff."

"But we didn't go last year," Jeremy said.

"Why not?" Fred interrogated.

"Well, trick-or-treatin' is really only for *little* kids," Boomer filled in.

"You passed up a chance to get lots of candy just because you thought you were too old?" Fred countered.

"Hmmm, when you put it that way, it does sound kind of dumb, doesn't it?" Boomer agreed.

"I haven't gone trick-or-treating in a long time," Marshall revealed. "In my old town, things were—" he paused, searching for the right words. "Well, no one cared about trick-or-treating; no one had time for it. My mom took me once when I was little, but other than that..." Marshall trailed off, not quite knowing how to finish.

"Wow," Sam said. "Even *my* parents let me go trick-or-treating. Sometimes my dad would even come with us."

"The only thing my dad does for Halloween is read. Every year, he reads the book *Frankenstein*,"

Marshall explained, shaking his head in a bewildered fashion.

"That's a book? I thought it was a movie!" Boomer questioned.

"But he's never gone trick-or-treating with me," Marshall reaffirmed.

"Well, that settles it," Boomer announced. "We've gotta go trick-or-treatin' so Fred and Marshall can have one good Halloween to remember."

Jeremy smiled weakly. "I don't know. I'd feel kind of silly dressing up in a costume."

"Oh, come on, it'll be fun," Boomer prodded. "We can go trick-or-treatin' and still have enough time to get over to that carnival. Mrs. Green said it's gonna start at seven."

Just then, Marshall sat upright. The conversation about trick-or-treating had completely distracted him from what he wanted to discuss. "Oh, that reminds me, speaking of the carnival—"

"Oh, not this again!" Jeremy interrupted. "I told you before, we can't win. The Benedict kids have too much money. You heard her," he pointed at Sam, "dunk tanks that someone's daddy is paying for. And that's just the 5th grade, no telling what the 6th graders are planning."

Sam shook her head. "They haven't come up with anything yet," she offered. "I heard Baxter talking about it yesterday."

Marshall grimaced, almost losing his nerve. He

turned to Sam, "But you said their parents pretty much buy off everything."

"I wouldn't be too sure. Whatever they do is bound to be pretty lame, just because they *think* their parents will bail them out. But a couple of nights ago, I overheard my mom saying that Baxter needed to learn some responsibility."

"So what's that mean?" Jeremy questioned.

"I know she's upset with Baxter. And I also know my dad wants this carnival to be a huge success, so it'll become a yearly tradition."

"Sounds like we should at least give it a shot," Marshall suggested. "What's the worst that could happen?"

Jeremy snorted. "We could waste a whole bunch of time and money and still end up getting trashed by Benedict. Why go through all that?"

"Well, what are we doing right now?" Marshall asked.

"Wastin' time," Boomer said with a look of dawning comprehension.

"Exactly," Marshall agreed.

"So, you got an idea?" Boomer questioned.

Marshall smiled. "Like I said earlier, last night while I was in bed, I was trying to think of something. But the more I thought about it, the more I kept coming up with nothing. Then, it hit me."

Boomer, John and Fred leaned forward expectantly.

"What kind of carnival is it?" Marshall quizzed.

"A Halloween carnival," Fred replied.

"Right," Marshall confirmed. "Now, all those other booths, balloons and darts, cakewalks, dunk tanks, a bingo-playing cow, the duck pond, those are all great, but in the end, they don't have anything to do with what?"

"Halloween," Jeremy answered, his curiosity peaking.

"Right," Marshall agreed. "So, what if our booth *did* have something to do with Halloween? Wouldn't that make it a bigger attraction?"

"Probably," Sam recognized.

"What'd you have in mind?" Boomer questioned.

Marshall smiled timidly, not sure how good of a plan it was. "A haunted house," he finally suggested.

"A haunted house?" Boomer repeated.

"Yeah, we can build a haunted house," Marshall explained. "Pick out a location, dress it up, and our class members could work inside, scaring people as they walked through."

"You know, that sounds like a swell idea," Boomer said excitedly.

John nodded rapidly in agreement.

"What do you think, Jeremy?" Boomer asked.

"Well, I still say it's a waste of time, because no matter what *she* says, I still don't think we can beat Benedict. But it definitely beats the duck pond," he conceded. "Where would we put it, though?" he pondered.

Marshall shrugged. "Let's take a look," he proposed.

They climbed the ladder to the second level and then the winding stairs leading to the turret above.

The view from above Radio Road proved even more impressive in the fall than it had been during the summer. The trees radiated with brilliant fall colors, the remaining leaves rustling in the breeze. Several people toiled with rakes in their yards, and one man with a hose struggled in vain to keep his grass alive.

Marshall focused his attention on the park, where small children played on the jungle gym. "It has to be a house close to the park," Marshall recommended.

Boomer motioned to a row of homes with backyards adjacent to the park. "Those people over there, I don't know any of them," he admitted.

"So, that leaves us with two options," Jeremy said in a resigned fashion.

Marshall pointed to the house on the west side of the park. It was an old, run down Victorian-style manor with high-peaked roofs. Rickety shutters hung off the windows and a rusty, iron gate stood in front of the walkway leading to the house. "That would be perfect, who lives there?"

"No chance!" Boomer exclaimed at once.

Jeremy nodded. "That's Eustace's place."

"Eustace?" Marshall thought for a moment, "the

janitor?"

"Yeah," Jeremy responded. "You've seen how he is; he hates kids."

Marshall's spirits deflated. The estate had the ideal appearance for a haunted house. "How did a janitor get a big, old house like that?" he inquired.

"My mom says he inherited it," Jeremy explained. "It's a real shame too; he's really let it go downhill. I guess it used to be the nicest house in the neighborhood." He shot a quick look at Sam before repeating, "Used to be."

"When? 1934?" Boomer quipped.

"Well, whose is this?" Marshall asked, pointing to the home on the east side of the park.

"Mine," Fred spoke up suddenly.

Marshall studied it, examining the possibilities. The house was not that impressive. In fact, it was very similar to the Beavers' home and all the others on this end of Radio Road. But it featured one interesting difference. One of the previous owners had built a garage, which was in the backyard and completely detached from the main structure. It was a decent-sized building, large enough for two cars.

"What about that garage?" Marshall wondered.

Boomer nodded. "That might work. Hey, Fred, could you ask your parents if we could use their garage for our haunted house?"

Fred rubbed his chin. "I guess I could—hey, wait a second!" he said suddenly. "Why should I help you guys? I'm not even in your class!"

"We'll take you trick-or-treating if you do," Marshall suggested.

Fred considered the proposition for a moment. "Oh, all right, I'll ask them," he agreed.

"Great!" Boomer said excitedly.

Jeremy smiled, but still seemed slightly apprehensive.

Marshall sighed. "Now all we have to do is get the others to go along with it."

Boomer slapped Marshall on the back encouragingly. "You leave that to me!"

7.

The Great Pumpkin Festival

Monday morning, Marshall woke with a sinking feeling in the pit of his stomach. He realized he would have to address the entire class and persuade them of his plan for the carnival. Convincing the guys in the tree house was one thing, but the whole class would be something else entirely. He got dressed and went downstairs for breakfast.

"Hurry up, I need to go," his mother encouraged.

"Uhh, actually, if it's all right with you, I think I'll walk to school this morning," Marshall responded. He wanted more time to consider the approach he would use, and now that the weather was cooler, the thought of walking to school didn't seem so bad.

His mother smiled enthusiastically. "It's all right with me," she returned. "Just make sure you give yourself plenty of time."

Marshall nodded and scooped a spoonful of

cereal into his mouth. He watched his mother gather her things and close the door behind her. As soon as she had left, he pushed the bowl away, having no appetite at all. He stood up and dumped the remaining cereal down the garbage disposal.

Ten minutes later, he stepped out the front door. As he turned onto the sidewalk, beginning the journey to school, his stomach churned. He made it to the end of the street and saw Boomer and John just leaving John's house.

"Hey, Marshall!" Boomer shouted as the two boys bounded across the road to join him. "Walkin' to school this morning? Ain't never seen you do that before."

Marshall stopped and waited as his friends approached. "So, did you spend the night at John's last night?" he asked.

Boomer laughed. "Nah, my mom works at the Save-Mart, pretty much all day. She drops me off at John's on her way to work, and I hang out there after school 'til it's time to go home."

"Hmm, do his parents get tired of you being there all the time?" Marshall questioned.

"Nah," Boomer corrected him. "You see, it's just John and his dad. And that's the beauty of it; I spend a lot of my time in the shop. I help his dad clean up and he teaches me how to fix cars. I've learned loads. He's an amazin' man," Boomer said, his eyes becoming misty.

"Sure sounds like it," Marshall responded,

absentmindedly kicking a rock in front of him.

"We was talkin' about that haunted house idea this morning," Boomer started. "So, you gonna bring it up today?"

Marshall missed the rock he had been kicking and halted in his tracks, the sinking feeling re-emerging in the pit of his stomach. Finally, he nodded reluctantly. "Yeah, I guess I'll have to," he acknowledged. "Since it's my idea."

"Don't you worry one little bit, we'll back you up."

"Thanks, Boomer," Marshall sighed.

They were nearly to school and Marshall's insides continued to tighten. He put a hand on his stomach.

"You gonna be sick, Marshall?" Boomer asked.

Marshall shook his head. "No, it's just nerves. The sooner this morning is over, the better."

As Marshall and the others opened the door to their classroom, they instantly noticed a change. The room had been decorated in orange and black, with pumpkins and black cats on the walls. Paper spiders and bats hung from the ceiling and a large cloth ghost lazily circled the classroom, attached to the ceiling fan.

The day started as every other, with Mrs. Green greeting them with a bright and cheery, "Good morning!"

"Good morning," the entire class responded.

"Oh, come on, we think you can do better than

that," Mrs. Green chided. "Good morning!"

"Good morning!" the class answered, louder this time.

"There we go," she said, clapping her hands together. "Now, the last instruction we gave you on Friday, we wanted you to come up with some ideas for our booth at the Halloween Carnival. So, did anyone think of anything?" she asked sweetly.

The entire class hemmed and hawed, a few stared down at their desks not wanting to be noticed, others shifted uncomfortably in their seats. Marshall was unsure of what to do.

The problem was quickly solved for him, though.

"Marshall's got a plan!" Boomer shouted. "And I think it's a dandy," he concluded, crossing his arms, as if that closed the book on the matter.

"Well, all right then!" Mrs. Green said, absolutely beaming. She turned towards Marshall. "Let's hear it!"

Marshall suddenly felt the strength give out in his legs. He doubted his ability to stand, but mustered his remaining courage and rose from his chair. He proceeded to explain the scheme as best he could, that since it was a Halloween-oriented event, the idea of a haunted house seemed natural. He also informed them that they had already scouted a perfect location to use. As he spoke, he tried gauging the reaction of his classmates, but he could interpret nothing. He finished to mixed reviews. Several of the boys seemed enthusiastic.

"Do you know how cool that would be?" one boy loudly whispered to his neighbor.

"Yeah, this is gonna be awesome!" said another.

"Well, I think it's great," Boomer concluded, making sure everyone heard him.

Three girls who sat rather close to Marshall; Brenda, Brittany, and Becky nodded in agreement. He could tell they liked the idea.

"It sounds dumb to me," muttered Jamie, one of the girls Marshall didn't know very well.

"Yeah, that's stupid," another girl named Jennifer agreed.

Katy, the girl sitting across from Marshall, turned and yelled across the room, "At least he suggested something you—"

"Okay, okay!" Mrs. Green interrupted, stepping forward. "Is Marshall's idea the only one we have? Does anyone else want to suggest something?"

No one said a word.

"All right, then," Mrs. Green continued. "Since this is a class project, we think the class should vote on it." She retrieved the sleek, black top hat from her desk and began handing out slips of paper which served as ballots. "We're going to leave the top hat right here. Just write YES if you *do* want to build the haunted house and NO if you *don't!* Everyone got that?"

The students rummaged through their desks and shuffled papers in an attempt to find a pen or pencil. Marshall received his own slip of paper and wrote "yes" and folded it. He joined the others as they stepped over to Mrs. Green's desk and deposited their ballots into the top hat.

Within moments, the voting was complete.

"Is that everyone?" Mrs. Green asked politely.

The students looked around and came to an agreement that everyone had voted.

Mrs. Green took out the pieces of paper and tallied the votes. "It looks like we have a winner, and by an overwhelming majority! 15-3 in favor of building a haunted house for the Halloween carnival!"

The class cheered and Marshall smiled, glancing at Jamie. She and Jennifer both sat back, their arms crossed in disgruntlement. Marshall couldn't help but wonder who the other dissenting vote had been.

The remainder of the morning breezed by. Marshall was so relieved to have the experience behind him, everything else seemed easy. As lunch approached, he realized just how hungry he was. The knot in his stomach had finally gone away, and he hadn't eaten any breakfast. His stomach grumbled as he eased back in his chair while Mrs. Green read *Sleepy Hollow* out loud to the class:

> *All the stories of ghosts and goblins*
> *that he had heard in the afternoon,*
> *now came crowding upon his*
> *recollection. The night grew darker*

> *and darker; the stars seemed to sink*
> *deeper in the sky, and driving clouds*
> *occasionally hid them from his sight.*
> *He had never felt so lonely and dismal.*

"All right! That's where we'll leave poor Ichabod Crane until after lunch!" she announced enthuseiastically.

The class groaned.

"Just one more page, Mrs. Green!" Boomer argued.

"But it's time to line up for lunch," Mrs. Green explained. She pulled out her top hat again and reached inside. "And this week, Boomer will be leading us to the lunch room!"

"Ahhh, Mrs. Green!" Boomer shouted. "Is my name the only one in that top hat?"

They lined up for lunch, as they did every day, and walked as a class towards the cafeteria. For some time now, Marshall had been eating the school lunches along with his companions. The cafeteria food wasn't the best in the world, but today, Marshall was starving. He sat next to Boomer and dug in. John, Jeremy, and Katy joined them shortly after.

"Don't worry about Jamie and Jennifer," Katy said, "they think *everything* is dumb unless one of them comes up with it."

"Yeah, Marshall," Boomer agreed. "Everyone else seemed to love the idea."

"Well, almost everyone," Jeremy said flatly.

"You know, I'm almost startin' to believe we can win this thing," Boomer added excitedly. "Every once in a while, I catch myself daydreamin' about how much fun that Wonderland amusement park is gonna be."

"How much fun it *would* be," Jeremy corrected. "I *still* don't think we can win."

"But just imagine," Boomer continued, paying no attention to Jeremy. "All them roller coasters and that log ride, the rapid river ride..." Boomer's voice faded off. He had a big smile on his face and seemed to be staring at something no one else could see. He absentmindedly dropped an elbow, catching the edge of his tray and rapidly flinging the contents into the air. They watched in horror as the food splattered all over John Beavers.

"Wow!" John exclaimed as macaroni and cheese fell from his hair.

"Oh no, John!" Mrs. Green cried from across the cafeteria. "Hurry off to the bathroom and see if you can clean up. Then go call your dad, maybe he can bring you some new clothes."

John left without a word.

"Poor kid," Katy commented, "seems stuff like that always happens to him."

They started eating again and Boomer was allowed to get a new tray. When he returned, he sat down and said, "So, Marshall, are you goin' to the–"

But Marshall didn't find out what he was supposed to be going to. John burst back into the lunch room, macaroni still dangling from his hair.

"*Phantom Plopper!*" he shouted with his arms extended into the air.

A roar erupted through the cafeteria as students began laughing and speculating about the identity of the culprit.

"Oh no, not again," Katy moaned dejectedly. She lowered her head, "That is soooo gross."

"Hey, at least you never have to see it, it's always in a boy's restroom," Jeremy countered.

Mrs. Green sighed, "Okay, we'll find Eustace and get him to clean it up–"

She hadn't even finished the sentence when a door behind the lunch counter lurched open. "Don't bother lookin' for me, Mrs. Green," a gravelly voice echoed as a hush fell across the cafeteria. "I'm right here."

"How does he do that?" Jeremy whispered.

Eustace's shaggy, gray hair hung down in his face and he pulled his mop bucket from the room he had just left. "You kids will be the death of me yet," he growled, wheeling the bucket behind him.

"Just go ahead and use the other restroom, John," Mrs. Green recommended.

John left again and Marshall remembered the conversation from earlier as the buzz died down. "Just a second ago, you were asking me if I was going somewhere," he prompted.

Boomer looked delighted. "Oh yeah! I was

gonna ask if you were goin' to the big punkin' carving festival?"

"Pumpkin carving festival?" Marshall questioned.

"Yeah, it's up at the Baptist church this weekend. None of us ever wins, but it's always a blast," Boomer explained. "They even give you a punkin' that you get to take home."

"I don't know, I'll have to think about it," Marshall said honestly.

The rest of the week passed without incident, and Friday after school, Marshall and the other boys went to the park to play the "keep away game." They'd had such a good time trying to keep the ball away from Baxter, Creature, and Ricky that they started playing the game on their own.

An hour later, they were thoroughly exhausted and Marshall had just announced he needed to get home.

"All right, but if you decide you want to go to the punkin' festival tonight, just head down to the church about six o'clock," Boomer hollered as Marshall ambled away.

Marshall hadn't been home long when his mother brought up the same topic. "I was talking to a couple of the other teachers and they were saying something about a pumpkin carving festival this evening. All the kids usually go and it's a lot of fun." She hesitated, as if waiting for Marshall to speak. "Does that sound like something you'd like to do?"

"Well," Marshall began slowly. "Not really, but Boomer's been talking about it, and you're going to make me go anyways, so I might as well just say I want to."

His mom laughed. "Wonderful, it starts at six o'clock, so you should have plenty of time to get ready."

Just before six that evening, Marshall and his mother left for the Baptist Church. They arrived to a parking lot jam-packed with cars.

"Looks like the whole town has turned out," his mom commented.

"No kidding," Marshall agreed.

Signs everywhere stated that the festival was being held outside, behind the church. So Marshall and his mother followed the signs around the building to discover a registration table with a nice, little lady smiling up at them. A basket filled with money sat on the edge of the table with a sign which read "Keep the Pumpkin Festival going, donations welcome".

The friendly woman asked for Marshall's name and age, so they knew which category to place his pumpkin in. After giving him a name tag, advisors ushered Marshall to a small mountain of pumpkins and instructed him to choose one. Marshall had never carved a pumpkin, so selecting the right one proved difficult.

His mother approached, pointing out pumpkins

and offering suggestions. "You want one with smooth sides, it'll be easier to carve," she advised. "Like that one over there, with the funny stem."

After what seemed like a lengthy process, Marshall finally picked out a nice-sized pumpkin. He searched around and found the table with Jeremy, Katy, Boomer, John, and Fred.

Boomer proudly showed Marshall his pumpkin. "I got here first, 'cause I wanted the best pick of the punkins."

"What are we supposed to do with this thing?" Fred asked, staring at the large orange object as if it had dropped down from a different planet.

Just then, Sam came trudging towards them, lugging a heavy pumpkin in her hands.

"Hey, Sam, I didn't expect to see you here," Marshall said.

"We come every year," Sam explained. "My dad believes it is part of his *civic duty* to be at these town-wide events like this."

Marshall panned the crowd, wondering who else might be there. The twins, Mike and David, sat at a table with Brenda, Brittany, and Becky. He spotted Baxter one row over, with Creature and Ricky planted on either side of him.

"What's *civic duty* mean?" Boomer questioned. But before Sam could reply, a voice on a microphone interrupted them.

"Welcome to the 20th Annual Radio Road Baptist Church Pumpkin Festival," a voice began. The man on the microphone thanked everyone for their generous donations and proceeded to explain the contest rules. "Now, begin your carving!" he concluded dramatically.

Plenty of adults stood by supervising the event. All of the carving was done with tiny saws, which were much safer than knives, but it still seemed dangerous enough. Marshall watched as Baxter pretended to stab his pumpkin with one of the saws, as if he were in a horror movie. An adult quickly reprimanded him and then explained the appropriate method of using the saw.

Marshall and his group managed to begin the process easily.

Fred peered inside his and shouted, "Oh, gross, these things stink!"

The insides of the pumpkin surprised Marshall as well. He had never seen one un-carved before.

They busily went to work scooping out the innards.

"Yuck, it's all slimy and slippery," Fred shouted, reaching into his for the first time.

Soon, a steadily growing mound of pumpkin innards filled the table between them.

"Now, we finally get to carve them," Sam said with a smile, wiping the sticky goo from her hands.

Marshall was no artist, but he was certainly familiar with the types of faces he had seen carved before. The church also had stencils available for elaborate carvings, which many of the older kids were using.

Marshall kept his simple, sketching a jagged mouth and triangle-shaped eyes before carving the face with his tiny saw. He compared his carving to those done by the others. The results satisfied him and he was glad to see his skills were not too far behind theirs.

Sam had done a more difficult carving, using one of the stencils, which took her longer to complete.

When the judges came by their table, they merely glanced at everyone's but Sam's. They paused and examined hers closely before continuing. Moments later, they came back and placed a 2nd place ribbon on it.

Sam frowned in disappointment, but followed with her eyes as they awarded first prize. They presented the blue ribbon to a boy several tables away.

"Mine's way better than his," Sam huffed.

Marshall leaned over to get a better view of the carving that won. It looked impressive to him, but he knew better than to say so. Just then, a sloppy glob smacked Marshall in the forehead. He reached up to discover pumpkin guts oozing down the side of his face.

He looked in the direction it had traveled from to find Baxter grinning evilly, more ammunition in hand, which he immediately launched at his sister.

Neither Sam nor Marshall hesitated. They each grabbed a handful of innards and heaved them towards Baxter. Marshall's hit the mark, but Sam's nailed Creature in the chest. This, of course, led to Creature seizing a wad of his own and flinging it towards them. Creature's throw missed wildly, splattering resoundingly across Boomer's face. Within seconds, a massive food fight ensued with sopping, soggy entrails flying in every direction.

Fred picked up an entire bowlful and dumped it on John's head. Creature and Ricky lobbed orange balls of glop at anyone foolish enough to open their mouth too wide.

Sam pulled on the back of Marshall's shirt and dropped a handful down the neck. He was thoroughly grossed out, yet, he was having the most fun he had ever had.

After what seemed like an eternity, the food fight died down and the man on the microphone formally announced the winners in every category. Following the announcement, much of the crowd dispersed. A few still lingered close by, including Baxter, who continuously motioned for his sister to hurry.

Marshall's mom joined them and tried to wipe the mess off his face. "You've never introduced me to all your friends," she said warmly.

Marshall was a bit embarrassed. "This is Sam," he introduced, pointing towards her, "she lives in the big house at the end of the street."

His mom raised her eyebrows and nodded in approval.

"This is Jeremy and Katy," Marshall continued, "and of course, Boomer you've met before. Over here is John Beavers, his dad owns the mechanic shop."

"And who is this?" his mother questioned, picking seeds out of Fred's hair.

Marshall smiled. "This is Chung-He Kim," he said, "he's from Korea."

Fred's jaw dropped. "You got it right!" he said excitedly.

Marshall laughed, "But we just call him Fred," he added. "We're building the haunted house for the carnival in his garage."

They all picked up their pumpkins, deciding to leave. As they traipsed around the church, they discussed the night's events, all of them still drenched in goop.

"I have to admit, that was a lot of fun," Marshall said through a grin.

"I think I have pumpkin guts in my pants!" Fred shouted.

Boomer beamed. "Yep, every festival has a different winner, but they all end up the same."

8.

The Save-Mart

The next several days could not pass quick enough. Most of the class was ecstatic about the carnival project, envisioning scary things the house might include. Their efforts hadn't proven very successful, but they received good news when Marshall's parents volunteered to help purchase the needed supplies.

It was the beginning of the third week of October and the boys were at the park playing yet another game of fast-paced keep away. Marshall had just caught the ball when his mom appeared around the corner.

"Marshall!" she called out. "Your father and I are going to the Save-Mart. Would you like to come along and buy your things for the carnival?"

The boys turned to each other in anticipation.

"Your friends can join us if they like," she added.

"All right!" Boomer said gleefully.

"We'll leave in about ten minutes," she said, smiling.

"Okay, mom," Marshall yelled back. "We'll be there in a second."

His mother acknowledged with a wave and disappeared again.

John and Boomer left to ask permission from John's dad.

"Let's take a look at Fred's garage," Marshall suggested to Jeremy. "I want to get a feel for what we might be able to use."

They walked the short distance from the park to Fred's house. His adopted parents had happily allowed them to use the garage. Marshall had hoped for a larger building, but this one would have to do.

A simple structure, the garage had paint peeling off the exterior, like so many other things on this end of Radio Road. A warped and rickety door hung loosely from rusty hinges, and shingles were missing in many places. However, none of this bothered Marshall, in fact, he thought it made the building more imposing.

Fred retrieved a key hidden inside a false rock in the bird bath. He opened the door and the others followed him inside to discover a considerable amount of junk piled to the ceiling.

"We'll have to move this stuff out, is that going

to be okay?" Marshall asked Fred.

"No problem," Fred replied. "He's got a big tarp that he'll put everything under during the carnival."

"Great," Marshall said, still surveying the surroundings. At one end of the structure, floorboards had been laid out across the rafters, allowing even more items to be stored. "Do you suppose that's sturdy enough to support someone?" Marshall wondered.

Fred looked frustrated. "How should I know, I've never been up there?"

Jeremy stepped to Marshall's side. "Well, right now there's several hundred pounds of stuff up there. No one in our class weighs that much," he offered, "except maybe Brenda."

Marshall laughed. "Good point," he admitted. "All right, I think we've seen all we need to. Let's find my parents."

They exited the garage and met Boomer and John at the door. Jeremy drifted away from the others, as if going back towards his own home.

"Aren't you comin' along, Jeremy?" Boomer questioned.

Jeremy shook his head. "Nah, you guys go ahead, I've got some things I need to do. You know, homework and stuff," he answered.

"Well, all right then, but you'll be missin' out on some fun," Boomer replied.

They waved goodbye to Jeremy and crossed Radio Road, making their way to Marshall's home.

Marshall's father waited in the car as his mother locked the front door behind her.

"We were just about to come find you," she said.

Dr. Maddox smiled brightly as the kids piled into the car. "You boys ready?" he asked.

"Sure thing, Mr. Marshall—I mean, Mr. Maddox, this is gonna be a blast," Boomer answered enthusiastically. "Maybe we'll see my mom," he added, "she works at the Save-Mart."

It was a tight fit, squeezing four kids across the backseat, but fortunately, John and Fred were rather small.

"So, are you guys excited about the carnival?" Marshall's mom questioned.

"You bet," Boomer replied. "Sounds like it'll be loads of fun. And Fred here ain't never celebrated Halloween 'cause of him bein' Chinese. So, that'll be fun too."

Fred drooped his head and sighed. "I keep telling you, I'm Korean!"

"You know, boys," Dr. Maddox interrupted, "Halloween is one of our oldest holidays. It was celebrated by the Celts in Ireland, as far back as three thousand years ago!"

The boys made the rest of the trip in silence, listening to Dr. Maddox explain the history of the holiday, but it wasn't long before they arrived at their destination. They spilled out of the car and onto the pavement. Quite a few vehicles filled the lot, as it was still early in the evening.

"Wow, sure is busy tonight," Marshall's mom observed.

"The Save-Mart's always busy," Boomer noted. "Mom's always complainin' about it."

The group walked through the automatic doors which slid open and dinged as they entered.

Boomer instantly scanned the row of checkout lines and started hollering, "Mom! Hey, Mom!" Half the women in line turned to look at him. Finally, his mother glanced up from her station and waved.

"That's my mom!" Boomer announced proudly, pointing towards her.

Marshall's dad smiled and acknowledged her as well.

"Hey, Marshall, you gotta come see something!" Boomer urged, turning his attention away from his mother.

Marshall hesitated for a moment. Running off from his parents in a crowded store was not something he was accustomed to. He glanced hopefully at his father who laughed.

"Go ahead," he encouraged. "We have some other shopping we need to do." He checked his watch. "We'll meet you in the Halloween department in fifteen minutes."

Marshall nodded and scrambled away with Boomer, John, and Fred. Boomer raced between the aisles until he found the correct one. The others almost had to run to keep up.

"Hold up," Boomer said, raising his hand. "This is what I was wantin' to show you."

They stopped in front of a display exhibiting the latest trendy brands of clothing. They all stared up at the arrangement.

"Huh," Marshall said in disbelief. "It really does look just like him."

In the center of the display stood a mannequin that looked exactly like Baxter Daniels. It had the same haircut, the same upturned nose, even the same smug expression etched on its face. It was similar in height to Baxter and even the clothes were remarkably like his normal attire.

"The Baxter dummy," Boomer whispered dramatically.

John reached his hand out, but Boomer pulled it back. "Don't touch it," he reprimanded.

The boys backed away from the mannequins and began wandering the store. They explored several different areas, first stopping in the pet department to examine the various kinds of fish. Then they checked out the sporting goods, inspecting the different equipment.

They spent several minutes in electronics, staring longingly at a brand new, pricey video game system. The boys then laughed uncontrollably after discovering they had drifted into the ladies' underwear department before eventually finding themselves back in the boys' clothing section.

Marshall looked up at a clock on the wall.

"Come on, guys, we need to get over to the Halloween Department."

Boomer and John gazed up at the dummy which bore such a striking resemblance to their neighborhood nemesis. "You go ahead," Boomer said slowly. "We'll catch up in a second."

Marshall walked away, followed by Fred.

"What's the big deal with that thing?" Fred asked.

"I have no idea," Marshall admitted.

Marshall and Fred maneuvered their way through the maze of aisles towards the Halloween items. His mom and dad were there already, examining a particularly gruesome-looking werewolf mask. "Who on earth would create such a thing?" Mrs. Maddox wondered aloud.

At the sight of Marshall and Fred, Marshall's father asked, "Where's the other two?"

Marshall shook his head. "They're–" he started, unsure how to explain. "They'll be here in a second," he finally said.

Marshall had barely finished the sentence when Boomer and John rushed around the corner, guilty expressions on their faces.

"Marshall!" Boomer bellowed.

"What?" Marshall said, exasperated.

"We didn't mean to do it, I swear we didn't," Boomer began.

Marshall's dad appeared concerned. "You didn't mean to do what?" he asked politely, approaching them.

"Well, we were standin' there lookin' at the Baxter dummy," Boomer started, still struggling to catch his breath.

"The what?"

Marshall shook his head, implying it would be best not to ask.

Boomer continued, "John poked the Baxter dummy. It wobbled back and forth for a second..." he didn't seem to have the heart to finish.

"Then what?" Marshall prompted.

"It fell over and—and—oh, Marshall, we broke the Baxter dummy! His head came clean off!"

Dr. Maddox frowned. He looked around, as if unsure of what to do. "Did anyone see you?" he interrogated.

Boomer shook his head.

He patted Boomer on the back. "Don't worry about it," he reassured. "I'm sure the Save-Mart has lots of mannequins, they'll probably be able to replace it."

This seemed to settle Boomer's nerves.

"Now," Dr. Maddox said energetically, "let's see what we can find!"

John instantly reached for the mask Marshall's mother had criticized earlier and slipped it on. He growled loudly, mimicking the sounds and gestures that werewolves typically make in movies.

"I love it!" Dr. Maddox shouted approvingly. "Throw it in the basket!"

John removed the mask and tossed it in the shopping cart.

"Hey, look at this!" Boomer said, waving a fake severed arm towards them.

"Fantastic!" Marshall's dad responded again.

Marshall's mother grimaced each time they chucked a grotesque item in the cart, but never complained.

Thirty minutes later, the shopping cart was brimming with all sorts of interesting things, from a plastic skeleton to tombstones they could prop up in the yard. They had also grabbed up several bags of cobwebs, some fake blood, scary masks, strobe lights, black lights, a fog machine, and various other devices to make the haunted house a roaring success.

After passing through the checkout line, they wheeled the shopping cart to the car and loaded the items into the trunk.

"Thanks a ton for gettin' all this stuff, Mr. Maddox," Boomer said.

"Yeah, thanks, Dad," Marshall agreed.

"Don't worry about it," his dad replied, reaching down and tousling Marshall's hair.

Marshall crawled into bed that night, barely able to sleep. It was almost like Christmas Eve. He knew that the next day they would begin making his dream a reality. Eventually he drifted off to sleep and woke up the next morning, eager to work.

Unfortunately, it would have to wait. After all,

they would be unable to do anything until after school. The boys spent the entire day recruiting help. Katy instantly agreed and so did David and Mike. CJ promised to show up and do whatever he could, and Mrs. Green announced she would help as soon as she left school.

They spent part of the afternoon setting up a work schedule on the chalkboard. Of course, Marshall, Boomer, and John volunteered to work every day. Jeremy said he would help out whenever he could, and almost everyone else signed up for at least one night during the week. The only holdouts were Jamie and Jennifer, the two girls who had been so critical of the plan. They absolutely refused to help with the project.

When the bell announced the end of the day, Marshall felt his confidence surging. The class seemed enthusiastic and anxious to work.

The four boys walked home in the cool autumn air, talking excitedly about their prospects.

"Man, I can't wait," Boomer said. "I can almost feel my stomach go up and down when I think about them roller coasters at Wonderland."

Jeremy snorted. "I still say our time would be better spent down at the arcade, or—anything else. You're forgetting about the Benedict kids," he said bitterly.

They retrieved the key from the rock and opened the garage door.

Marshall examined the work that lay before

them. "Okay," he said, "first thing we have to do is move all of this stuff out."

They began the tedious process of lugging items outside. Fred's adopted parents had lived in the house for decades. They had collected more possessions than one could imagine. Nothing seemed really valuable, Marshall noticed as he passed items down from the rafters, just a lot of it.

There was a wide variety too, from old life preservers, to fishing lines, poles, and nets. Assorted tools of every kind littered the walls and an old, emerald-green raincoat hung from a hook. They also uncovered an ice chest with an extensive crack in the lid, several dusty mirrors, and some sort of contraption Marshall had never seen before.

"You reload shotgun shells with that thing there," Boomer explained as Marshall examined the strange device.

"I see," Marshall responded, picking it up carefully.

As they worked, more and more classmates arrived. Together, they toiled tirelessly into the late evening, cleaning out the garage. By the time they had completed the task, full darkness had set in.

"Boy howdy, that sure was a lot of work," Boomer stated, dusting his hands off.

"Yeah, and we haven't even started the decorating yet," Jeremy observed, picking a cobweb out of his hair.

On the second day, Mrs. Green helped them

hang black tarps and trash bags over the walls and even the ceiling, providing the entire garage with the proper atmosphere. They rigged up clotheslines and created a walk through maze with black tarp and more trash bags.

John brought some tattered beige coveralls he had borrowed from his dad. They stuffed the outfit full of newspapers, creating a fairly convincing scarecrow. John even had an old space helmet they used as the head.

Brenda, Brittany, and Becky had fun stringing cobwebs over every inch of the garage, both inside and out. They placed the tombstones outside the door where guests would enter, and set up a table for CJ to take tickets.

"Why do we have these?" Katy asked, staring down at the pile of rubber masks.

Marshall laughed. "Pretty much the only thing that'll scare anyone in here will be us. We'll be dressed in these masks," he said picking one up. "When someone comes around a corner, we'll jump out and scare them." He dropped the mask back on the pile. "Startle them is probably a better word," he added philosophically.

Towards the end of the week, as they made the final adjustments, Sam came to visit.

"What do you think?" Marshall asked, desiring her approval.

She smiled meekly. "It's great, only–"

"Only what?" Marshall prodded.

Sam seemed uncomfortable. "I just found out something, and I thought you guys ought to know."

"Thought we ought to know what?" Jeremy asked, coming up beside them.

A few others gathered around.

Turning away from the group, Sam inspected the garage again. "My brother and his class," she began, "they're doing the same thing."

"What do you mean?" Marshall interrogated.

"This," she said, waving a hand around. "They're building a haunted house, just like you guys."

Marshall closed his eyes and released a long, slow breath.

"I knew it," Jeremy growled. "Total waste of time. Ours will be pathetic compared to theirs."

Marshall shook his head. The cloud he'd been riding for the last week seemed to evaporate beneath his feet. "I don't get it," he finally said. "How did they–" he looked at Sam, not wanting to say what he was thinking. "You didn't–"

"Of course she did," Jeremy scoffed. "As soon as she heard your big idea in the tree house, she probably went and blabbed the whole thing."

Sam scowled heatedly. "I never said a word to Baxter. I barely even talk to him."

"Yeah, right," Jeremy sneered sarcastically.

Sam turned to Marshall, seeking support. "I promise, I didn't," she pleaded.

Marshall glared at Jeremy, anger swelling inside. He forced himself to remain calm. "There must be another explanation. Two different groups could come up with the same idea, couldn't they?" he reasoned.

"So, now what do we do?" Jeremy questioned.

Marshall shrugged. "The only thing we can do," he suggested. "We finish. We finish just like we planned and do the best we can."

They concluded their preparations, trying not to imagine how much better the Benedict haunted house would be than theirs.

After a solid week of working every evening, they had finished. The others had gone home already, and Marshall, Jeremy, Boomer, John, and Fred were admiring their work.

"Sure looks good doesn't it?" Boomer stated proudly.

Marshall smiled. It wasn't exactly what he had envisioned, but it was the best they could do. "It sure does," he said aloud.

"This calls for a celebration!" Boomer declared.

"What did you have in mind, Boomer?" Jeremy asked.

"I think it's time for a good old-fashioned sleepover in the tree house."

"Sleepover?" Marshall questioned.

Jeremy, John, and Boomer smiled and nodded.

"Sleepover it is," they said together.

9.

The Sleepover

Marshall raced home to ask permission to spend the night in the tree house. He had never been to a sleepover before. In his old town, the concept of a sleepover would have seemed unsafe or old fashioned.

"A sleepover?" his mom questioned when he proposed the issue. "I don't know, it's getting pretty cool at night, and I'm sure that tree house is drafty."

Marshall shook his head. "It's really well-built, it has electricity and everything," he argued.

"Wow, sounds like I'll have to come see that," his dad said in amazement.

Marshall directed his focus on his father, sensing

a window of opportunity. "John's dad built it. They say he's a real wiz." He paused for a moment, "So, can I go?" he asked again, pleading to his dad.

"Sure, why not?" Dr. Maddox replied. "Sounds like fun to me, just don't get into any trouble."

"We won't," Marshall assured him.

After scarfing down his dinner, he hurried up to his room. He wasn't exactly sure what he would need, so he packed a few items and retrieved his sleeping bag from the top part of his closet. He then sat and waited in anxious anticipation as the minutes crawled by.

At 8:00 sharp, Marshall picked up his bags and trampled down the stairs.

"I'm gonna go now," Marshall shouted to his parents.

"Okay, have a good time," his father encouraged, glancing up from a thick novel.

"If it gets too cold, you come home," his mother declared. "I don't want you getting sick."

"All right," Marshall agreed. "Thanks for letting me go," he added.

He stepped outside and scrambled through the darkness in the direction of the Beavers' home. Rounding the corner, the sight of a warm glow radiating from the tree house windows captured his attention. Boomer's carved pumpkin peaked through the glass, a candle flickering from within. Marshall stopped in his tracks, smiling at the inviting scene.

He ascended the stairs and knocked. The knob turned and the door swung upwards as Boomer greeted him with a smile.

"Heck, Marshall," Boomer started, "you don't need to knock anymore; you're just one of the guys. I mean, it ain't like we're sittin' around in our underwear or anything."

Fred and John were rooted in their usual spot on the couch, absorbed in a video game. Jeremy didn't seem to be there at all.

"Where's Jeremy?" Marshall wondered.

Boomer shrugged. "I don't rightly know. I suppose he'll be here before long."

Marshall and Boomer settled in, watching John and Fred battle each other on the screen. Fred won, jumped up and performed a small celebration.

"Thirty games in a row!" Fred cheered before tallying a point on a small marker board.

"Let me give it a whack," Boomer volunteered.

At that moment, the door swung open and Jeremy entered.

"Where ya been?" Boomer questioned.

Jeremy shook his head. "Ahh, I had some stuff to do," he responded without further explanation.

"I's just gettin' ready to take on Fred at this here game," Boomer informed as Jeremy joined the group.

Together, the boys relaxed and watched as Fred clobbered Boomer. Jeremy tried next and lost miserably as well.

"Come on, Marshall, you're up!" Boomer prodded.

"But I've never played this game before!" Marshall protested.

"Well, there's no better time to start," Boomer continued.

Marshall reluctantly agreed and took the controller in hand. He had played many other games which were much more challenging, but Fred had a knack for this one. For quite a while, it appeared Marshall could win, but in the end, Fred pulled out another victory.

"Wow, Marshall, that was darn good for a beginner," Boomer said in an impressed tone.

Marshall smiled awkwardly, uncomfortable accepting compliments. He rose from the couch and John replaced him.

The evening commenced with Fred extending his winning streak to fifty-one in a row. Marshall came close on a couple of attempts, but somehow, Fred always won.

Marshall and Jeremy tired of the process and went upstairs to pick out a few board games. They returned and had just sat down at the table when the door suddenly swung open. Sam and Katy lumbered into the tree house, toting along a big bag full of–something.

"What're you two doing here?" Jeremy asked, a hint of irritation in his voice.

"Well, hello, Sam, Katy!" Boomer greeted enthusiastically.

"Hey, Boomer," the girls replied.

Sam turned to Jeremy and responded. "I'm spending the night at Katy's. We were out walking and saw the lights on up here." She took a seat next to Marshall and smiled.

Marshall grinned in return. "What's in the sack?" he asked.

She giggled. "Oh, that's for later."

Marshall didn't bother pursuing the issue. "We were just getting ready to play a game, you want to join us?" he invited.

"Sounds like fun," Katy agreed, playfully nudging Jeremy as she nestled in beside him on the long bench.

Boomer came over as well, and the five of them happily played *Clue*, a checkers tournament, and then a very brief game of *Monopoly* as the hours trickled by. They enjoyed themselves, laughing at Boomer's reaction as he landed on Boardwalk for the fifth time. The group poked fun at each other, their classmates, teachers, and the other school employees.

"So, what do you suppose Eustace does in that closet all day?" Jeremy asked the group as a whole.

"I heard he and the lunch lady go in there and smooch," Boomer suggested. "Have you seen the way they look at each other in the lunchroom?"

"I think it's his office," Marshall suggested reasonably.

"Who has an office in a closet?" Jeremy asked, bewildered.

"Okay, I got me an idea," Boomer said. "Let's play a different kind of game. Let's say we all have to go around the circle and say one thing that no one else knows."

"Who are you, Mrs. Green?" Jeremy chided.

"You mean like Truth or Dare?" Sam offered, her eyes widening.

Boomer wrinkled his nose. "Well, sort of, but I'm not too sure about the darin' part." He thought about it for a moment and then added, "I'll go first."

Before Boomer could say anything, Jeremy interrupted. "Wait a second. Marshall, Sam, and Fred have an unfair advantage here. I mean, the rest of us know almost everything about each other."

"Oh, I bet you don't know everything about *me*," Katy laughed.

"But that's what made me think of this," Boomer explained. "I figured it'd help us get to know each other."

"All right, we'll give it a shot," Jeremy said reluctantly.

Boomer considered his words for a moment before saying, "Okay, before my dad died—I was only about four at the time—we used to have a big ranch with about twenty horses and all sorts of cattle. Now, we only got the two horses that y'all know, ol' Sunspot and Moonbeam."

Jeremy seemed impressed. "Wow, I never knew that," he said mildly.

"Yep," Boomer went on, "Mom had to sell all the cattle, she couldn't work 'em herself, you know. She'd never had to work before, but now she works at the Save-Mart."

"John, your turn," Jeremy suggested.

John pulled his eyes from the television screen and stared at them. "What?"

"One thing no one in this room knows about you?" Jeremy explained.

John thought about it for a moment. "In 1st grade, Creature and I used to be best friends. His real name is Marion."

The entire room broke into laughter.

"You've got to be kidding me," Jeremy laughed.

Marshall shook his head. "I can't see it," he agreed.

"No wonder he goes by Creature," Katy chuckled.

"He was a lot smaller then," John continued.

"All right, Fred, your turn," Boomer said.

"Ahhh, I don't know what to tell you guys," Fred returned.

"Come on, tell us how you got to America," Boomer prompted.

Fred paused the video game and set the controller aside. "How I got to America?" he started, but then stopped.

The others quieted down, sensing the seriousness in Fred's demeanor.

"My father was arrested by the North Korean government when I was five. I never saw him again," Fred began. "My mother was really sick, and she didn't want me growing up in North Korea, so we escaped." He hesitated, staring deeply into the television screen. "The escape was too much for her. I was found on the side of the road, my mother beside me." He turned back towards them before finishing. "I ended up in a South Korean orphanage for four years before I was adopted and sent to the United States." He picked up the controller to continue his game. "That's how I got here."

They all sat, stunned by what he had just told them.

"Wow," Sam finally whispered.

Boomer, caught in a rare speechless moment, swallowed hard.

The faint sounds of the video game ended the silence as Fred and John resumed playing.

"Marshall, I guess it's your turn," Jeremy said, trying to break the somber mood.

Marshall gave a small laugh. "There's no way I can top that one," he said.

"Let me guess, you were some sort of all-star quarterback on your old little league team, weren't you?" Jeremy taunted.

Marshall shook his head. "No, actually, I played soccer."

"Soccer?" Boomer asked in amazement. "Why

would anyone wanna–"

"And he was probably brilliant at that too," Jeremy said sarcastically.

Marshall laughed. "Okay, let's see–when I first heard my dad had gotten a job here, I seriously didn't want to move. I thought this was like, some sort of backwoods, redneck-type place."

"Well, we love you too," Jeremy said defensively.

Marshall held up his hands, "I don't think that now–" he started.

"We know what'chya mean Marshall, it's all right," Boomer said. "Sam, you're up!"

Sam tugged at her bottom lip and seemed to be deliberating over her answer. "Hmmm, Jeremy, you're always calling me a spoiled rich girl, so you might appreciate this. I have never cooked or baked anything in my life," she admitted.

Jeremy laughed, as if this confirmed his worst fears.

"Never cooked anything?" Boomer responded, perplexed. "Jeez, my mom's cookin' stuff every night!"

"Okay, I helped make Jell-O one time at my Aunt Margaret's house, but that's it," Sam offered.

"Jell-O?" Marshall repeated, laughing.

"Margaret? How old is she? A hundred?" Jeremy teased.

Katy shot a disapproving glance in Jeremy's direction and nudged him in the side. "That's not very nice," she said lightheartedly.

"You have an Aunt Margaret?" Boomer asked, overly enthused. "Well, I got me an Aunt Margaret too!"

"She's actually my mother's *little* sister," Sam explained to Jeremy. She then shifted her attention towards Katy. "Okay, your turn," she prompted.

Katy buried her face in her hands. "This summer, Baxter and I kissed each other," she mumbled as she turned beet red.

"Wow!" Boomer exclaimed, "Now there's something you can't do with the Baxter dummy!" He thought for a moment, a hand on his chin. "Well, I guess you could, but—"

Sam looked appalled. "Oh, please tell me that's not true! Katy how could you?" she groaned.

Marshall laughed as well.

Jeremy rubbed his head and leaned forward. He appeared to be brooding, but said nothing.

"When did this happen?" Sam interrogated.

"At camp… in July," Katy answered.

They joked for another moment, considering what they had just learned.

"All right, Jeremy, you're last," Marshall urged.

Jeremy straightened up in his chair. "Boomer and John, you know the first half of this," he began. "My mom used to be a clown. That's what she did for a living, she was in a circus. But the part you don't know is that sometimes, when I was younger, she—" he stopped as if he couldn't bring himself to finish.

"She what?" Boomer encouraged.

Jeremy shook his head. "No, I can't say it, just forget I mentioned it."

Katy wrapped an arm around his shoulder. "Oh, come on, it can't be any worse than what I said."

Jeremy took a deep breath and pressed on. "She would sometimes dress me up in a clown costume and make me perform with her," he said all in one breath.

Again, everyone in the room roared with laughter.

"I had no idea," Boomer chuckled. "Jeremy the Clown!"

"My brother's afraid of clowns," Sam told them in between giggles.

"Well, I can't say I'm too fond of 'em myself," Boomer agreed. "John, what do you think?"

John shook his head. "Clowns smell funny."

"See, that wasn't so bad, was it?" Katy commented, patting Jeremy's shoulder.

"Oh, by the way," Sam said suddenly. "Speaking of my brother, that reminds me," she reached down and grabbed the bag on the floor. She began removing roll after roll of toilet paper and placing them on the table.

"Toilet paper reminds you of your brother?" Marshall asked.

"Makes sense to me," Jeremy quipped.

Sam and Katy both giggled.

Boomer picked up a roll and examined it intently. "Boy, this sure is some quality stuff."

"What are we supposed to do with these?" Marshall questioned.

"We can TP my house," Sam volunteered.

"Your house?" Jeremy repeated. "You want *us* to TP the nicest house in the county?"

"Well, I *am* going with you," she pointed out. "So, if we get caught, it's no big deal. And if we don't get caught," a mischievous grin crossed her face, "guess who gets to clean it up tomorrow?"

"Baxter?" Marshall said with a smile.

"Baxter," Sam agreed.

"Well, all right," Boomer chuckled, "sounds like a plan to me!"

It was well past midnight, so they opened the door and quietly slipped outside. The deadly stillness of the neighborhood unnerved Marshall as they crept their way up Radio Road. In his old town, vehicles were always coming and going, even at this hour of the night.

"Man, that place is really spooky," Jeremy whispered, gesturing towards the dilapidated manor towering above the wrought-iron fence.

"Yeah, it's always given me the creeps," Katy acknowledged as the rusty gate creaked on its hinges.

They stealthily made their way towards the enormous house at the end of the street, Boomer tugging along the big sack of toilet paper he had volunteered to carry.

Standing in front of the Daniels' home, roll of toilet paper in hand, Marshall couldn't help but feel guilty. He had certainly never TP'd someone's house before, and Mr. Daniels had been so nice to him when they had met. Then, he thought of Baxter and suddenly felt a lot less guilty.

Sam heaved the first roll high in the air, and it slung itself over a tree branch and came streaming back to the ground. Jeremy and Boomer joined in, tossing their paper rolls in the air like pros. They obviously had more experience.

Marshall gave it a shot. It wasn't as easy as Sam made it look, but his roll came down safely.

Fred attempted to throw his and the roll left his hand, smacking against the roof of the house.

"Watch it," Sam whispered. "That was right over my parent's bedroom."

"You gotta put backspin on it, Fred," Jeremy suggested.

"What's backspin?" Fred asked.

"It's a shame to waste such fine toilet paper on a house," Boomer said regretfully, rearing his arm back for another toss.

Several minutes later, with the trees and front porch thoroughly covered in toilet paper, they ran away laughing, glancing back and admiring their handy work.

"Hey, while we're out, why don't we slip down to the shop and grab us somethin' to drink," Boomer suggested. "Mr. Beavers has always got the fridge stocked with tons of sody pop."

They all agreed, and Marshall admitted interest in seeing this place he had heard so much about.

It was a long walk back down Radio Road. As they neared Fred's home, Marshall suddenly halted, believing he'd heard the sound of snarky laughter.

"What was that?" Marshall gasped.

"What?" the girls asked together.

Marshall shook his head. "I thought I heard something," he said.

Sam and Katy glanced around nervously.

"Oh, stop trying to scare them," Jeremy admonished, motioning to the others.

Jeremy led the way as they resumed their journey, but a few steps later, Marshall stopped again, catching sight of a long, slender shadow cast by the street light.

"Did you see that?" Marshall exclaimed, pointing.

Jeremy seemed anxious. "Seriously, Marshall, cut it out," he argued.

"Probably just a cat, Marshall," Boomer suggested.

Marshall shook his head and blinked hard, attempting to focus through the darkness. He started to wonder if the Halloween atmosphere of late October was affecting him.

"Let's just get to the shop," Sam prompted.

The Beavers' Mechanic Shop was an old building that had the appearance of a gigantic tin can turned on its side. A sign over the door read:

BEAVERS MECHANICS SHO

Marshall assumed the *P* had fallen off at some point in the past. He stared back through the shadows lurching across Radio Road as Boomer worked at the combination lock holding the doors together. A satisfying click granted them entry and Boomer quietly slid the doors open enough to slip through. Once inside, John stepped into the office and switched on the lights.

The entire garage lit up around them. Marshall and Sam drifted away from the group, inspecting the wide array of contraptions while the others marched on to the refrigerator.

A large cabinet resembling a salad bar sat against the far wall. Holes cut from the top served as bins where Mr. Beavers kept his tools. Several pairs of long rubber gloves hung on the wall along with an assortment of ropes, pulleys, and other devices Marshall couldn't even imagine a use for.

Of course, two or three cars filled the middle of the garage, various engine parts littering the floor around them. Lawn mowers, washing machines, and other mechanical objects cluttered every other inch of the concrete slab.

"I see he works on more than just cars," Marshall observed.

Sam nodded. "Even my dad says he's a genius

who can fix anything."

"No wonder Boomer admires him so much," Marshall admitted.

"Here you go, Marshall, Sam," Boomer said, startling them from behind. He handed a bottle of soda to each of them. "This is quite a place, isn't it?" Boomer said, raising his own drink towards the ceiling.

"It sure is," Marshall agreed as he approached a couple of wrecked bicycles.

"Yep, me and John's bikes," Boomer acknowledged, raising his eyebrows. "John's dad hasn't gotten around to fixin' those yet."

"What happened to them?" Sam questioned.

Jeremy stepped closer to them and started in, "Well, you see, there was this day last summer when Boomer had the brilliant idea to–"

"Now, don't go bringin' that back up," Boomer interrupted, cutting off his friend, "the less said about that day, the better." Boomer ran his fingers through his bristly hair and cleared his throat. "Allow me to show you some of the finer points of this facility," Boomer offered, sounding like a waiter in a fancy restaurant.

He approached what appeared to be a simple rack of tools. But Boomer flipped a switch and the rack revolved a third of the way around, revealing an entirely different selection of tools. He punched the button once more and yet even more tools appeared.

"That's amazing," Marshall commented.

"Yeah," Boomer agreed, "he rigged this up himself. Also did all the wirin' on his sound system," he said, pointing towards the ceiling.

Marshall looked around and spotted several speakers throughout the building.

"He likes to listen to music while he works," Boomer explained.

Boomer showed off a few more items of interest before they decided to head back to the tree house. They locked up and slipped around the corner towards the Beavers' backyard.

Sam and Katy realized it was way past time for them to be home, and they hoped Katy's parents hadn't noticed how long they had been gone. They said their goodbyes and disappeared up Radio Road.

The guys went back to the tree house and played several more rounds of video games. Later, they warmed up frozen pizzas in the microwave and sat eating them while guzzling down even more soda. As the night slipped by, Boomer, Jeremy, and Marshall exchanged their best ghost stories as *Dracula* played silently on the television.

Finally, as the predawn hours crept up on them, they decided to call it a night, overcome by exhaustion. They climbed to the second level where the four cots and hammock waited. Jeremy called the hammock, relegating the others to cots. Marshall unrolled his sleeping bag onto one of the cots as the other boys did the same.

It had been a fun day, but a long one. Marshall fell asleep almost as soon as his head hit the pillow.

10.

The Accusation & The Confession

"Marshall! Marshall! Wake up!" Fred's voice echoed through Marshall's peaceful sleep.

"Boomer, Jeremy, wake up!" Fred shouted again.

"What is it, Fred?" Marshall finally asked, coming to his senses.

"Something terrible has happened, you won't believe it!" he yelled as he started down the ladder.

Marshall jumped to his feet as Boomer did the same. He hadn't known Fred for long, but from the tone of his voice he knew something was very wrong.

They hustled down the ladder of the second deck, swung the door open and descended the steps as Fred waved from his backyard. Marshall clambered over the chain-link fence separating the two yards and walked briskly towards the garage.

"Look!" said Fred, pointing into the garage.

Marshall and Boomer peered through the door and gasped. Everything was trashed. All of the bags and tarps had been ripped from the walls. The scarecrow made from Mr. Beavers' old clothes had been torn apart and scattered everywhere. Most of the decorations the girls had labored so hard on during the week had been stripped down and mangled. Many items were smashed beyond recognition. The masks his parents had purchased were sliced to pieces.

Just then, Jeremy joined them and gazed at the destruction. He nervously stepped inside and began investigating the damage.

"Who would do this?" Marshall asked, still absorbing the devastation.

"It was them Benedict kids, it had to be," Boomer suggested.

"But surely they wouldn't–" Marshall trailed off, unsure how to finish.

Jeremy raised one of the trash bags for Marshall to examine. A large "B" had been emblazoned across it with green spray paint.

"Does that answer your question?" Jeremy asked. "B for Benedict. It's even in their school colors" he added.

"Or B for Baxter," Marshall deduced. "Where's John?"

"He went to tell the others," Fred said.

As if on cue, Brenda, Brittany, and Becky

rounded the corner with shocked expressions.

"John just told us," Brenda said. "Is it true?" she asked dispiritedly.

Marshall stepped aside and allowed the newcomers to view the disaster for themselves.

"Oh my gosh!" Brittany whispered.

"I can't believe it," Becky croaked.

"All that work we did, all week long," Brenda sniffed.

Jeremy hoisted the bag a second time to present the venomous green B.

Brittany snatched the piece of plastic and studied it. "But how did they get in?" she wondered aloud. "Wasn't the door locked?"

Becky jerked the bag from Brittany's hand. "It must've been that girl, Sam. She must've blabbed to her brother—" she started, glaring at Marshall accusingly.

Marshall shook his head. "I don't think Sam said anything," he responded defensively.

"Oh, come on, Marshall, isn't it obvious?" Brittany snapped.

Marshall turned to Boomer, hoping for support.

Boomer shrugged. "I'm afraid I have to agree with 'em, Marshall. Sure seems like that charmin' temptress led us astray." He scratched his head as if deep in thought. "She lured us out with them big, bright, shiny rolls of toilet paper—then, while we was away, Baxter and his thugs did this."

Marshall stood motionless, stunned into silence.

Boomer continued. "She knew where we was settin' it all up, she knew where the key was, and she led us away from the scene of the crime."

At that moment, Sam, Katy, and John burst around the corner, huffing for breath.

"What happened?" Sam asked.

"As if you don't know," Becky said scathingly.

"What do you mean?" Sam questioned, gazing around.

"Oh, don't act like you're shocked," Brenda snarled, closing the distance between them.

"But I didn't–you don't think I–what's going on?" Sam stammered, retreating backwards.

"They think you told your brother how to get in," Marshall explained, stepping between the two girls.

"But I was with you last night," she said, turning to both Marshall and Katy in desperation.

"Oh, that's a convenient excuse," Brittany muttered.

"I know you were, but that wouldn't prevent you from telling Baxter where to find the key," Marshall admitted.

Sam turned to Marshall, exasperated. "*You* don't think I had anything to do with this?"

Marshall grimaced. He kicked one of the tombstones that had been pulled from the ground. "I'm not sure what to think anymore."

Sam fell back to Katy as her last line of defense. "You know I wouldn't do that," she pleaded.

Katy smiled weakly, but didn't respond. She

sidled closer to Jeremy who stared resolutely at the ground.

"Well, I think she would," Becky barked, raising a hand towards Sam, as if preparing to slap her.

"She didn't," Jeremy said finally, charging in front of Sam.

Marshall had nearly forgotten him. Jeremy had been suspiciously quiet during the accusations of Sam, considering he had so willingly criticized her before. "What do you mean, she didn't?" Marshall demanded.

Jeremy shook his head. "She didn't have anything to do with it."

"How do you know?" Katy challenged.

Jeremy's expression soured. "Because I did it." He stopped for a moment as they stared in disbelief. "I mean, I didn't do this," he explained, motioning towards the mess, "I told Baxter where the key was."

Marshall frowned with despair. He could think of nothing to say except, "But why?"

"Because–" Jeremy began, but stopped. He turned away and flung out a hand, "I don't know." Jeremy stepped into the garage, shuffling junk with his feet as he moved. "I knew we'd lose and look like fools. So, I thought if they came in here and trashed a bunch of stuff, you guys would give up."

"Well, it worked," Katy said, her face reddening with anger. She approached Sam and placed a hand on her shoulder. "There's no way we can put it back together now."

Jeremy sighed remorsefully. "But I didn't think they would go this far," he admitted, waving a hand in frustration. "I just wanted them to knock things down, take things apart. I didn't tell them to wreck the place."

"That's my brother for you," Sam said. "Give him an inch, and he won't only take a mile, but he'll take the mile and smash it into a million pieces." She looked around to the others. "Trust me, he wanted to do this long before Jeremy ever gave him the opportunity. So don't blame Jeremy too much."

Katy strode towards Jeremy. "Is that why they're building a haunted house too? Did you tell them?" she interrogated.

"No," Jeremy sighed. "He overheard Marshall say something at the Pumpkin Festival. That's how they got the idea." He lowered his head and trudged through the crowd without saying a word, sulking towards his own home.

Marshall watched as Jeremy drifted away. Turning back to the group, Marshall asked, "So, what do we do now?"

"What do we do?" Katy repeated. "We go home! There's no way we could do this again, all of our stuff is ruined."

"Come on, guys, we built it once in a week, so we can build it again in a week," Marshall encouraged. "Just give me a day or two, I'll find a way to keep us in this carnival."

"We're all behind ya', Marshall," Boomer encouraged, "but we just don't see how it's possible. All them things your parents bought for us," he said, kneeling down and scooping up half of the werewolf mask John had worn at the Save-Mart. "It's all gone," he concluded, his hand trembling as he held out the mask.

"Just give me time," Marshall implored, "I promise, I won't let you down."

That afternoon, Marshall poured over the problem in his mind. The day was dark and overcast. Sometime about mid-afternoon, it began to rain and Marshall listened to the drops hitting the roof as he sat at his desk, contemplating.

He laid out blank pieces of white paper and began doodling. The doodles turned into rough sketches. The rough sketches turned into diagrams. The diagrams turned into blue prints. He had some good ideas, but was unsure if they would work. Also, there still seemed to be something missing, an angle he hadn't yet discovered.

The rain had not yet let up when he ventured downstairs for dinner that evening. He knew that his parents could tell he was upset, but he just couldn't bring himself to inform them that all the items they had bought for his class, all the money they had spent, had been for nothing.

"Everything all right?" his dad asked towards the end of dinner.

"What? Oh yeah," replied Marshall, his mind so distracted he had barely heard the question.

"Sure doesn't seem like it," his dad speculated, studying him closely.

"I'm fine," Marshall lied.

"Well, if anything's ever bothering you, you know you can talk to me," his father said kindly.

Marshall nodded and excused himself from the table. He went back to his bedroom and returned to his desk, listening to the sound of the rain patting against the roof. He began mulling over what his dad had just said.

"That's the last thing I need," he muttered aloud. He laid his head on the desk. "Being analyzed by my psychology professor father like I'm a patient or something."

Marshall bolted upright as if lightning had struck him. "Wait a second–" he murmured, rolling the idea over in his mind. "That's it!" he exclaimed.

He stood up and raced down the stairs to find the table cleared and his father already in his office. He rarely disturbed his dad there, but right now, Marshall didn't care. Tonight, he wanted his father's advice more than he had ever wanted it before. He timidly stepped into the doorway and cleared his throat.

Dr. Maddox looked up from the book he was reading. "Well, hello, Marshall," he said kindly.

"Still reading *Frankenstein*?" Marshall asked, noticing the novel in his father's hand.

"Absolutely," Dr. Maddox acknowledged. "You know, Mary Shelley was only eighteen when she wrote this." He placed a bookmark between the pages and set the book down on his desk. "So, what brings you in here?"

"I need your help, Dad," Marshall began. "I need you to tell me what people are afraid of."

The following day, Marshall left for the tree house just after lunch, with several pieces of paper clutched in his hand. Sam met him at the edge of the sidewalk.

"I see you got my message," Marshall said with a smile.

"Yep," Sam replied. "What's this all about?"

Marshall waved the papers in his hand. "I'll show you in just a second."

It was a Sunday afternoon, and he was positive the guys would be there already. Sure enough, as they approached, he spotted Boomer through the window. Likewise, Boomer saw them and waved. Marshall and Sam returned the gesture and by the time they arrived at the foot of the stairs, Boomer had already opened the door in anticipation.

"Hey, Marshall, what's goin' on?" Boomer questioned.

"I've got some stuff to show you guys. I worked on this all day yesterday," Marshall said enthusiastically.

Boomer, John, Fred, and Sam gathered around

the table as Marshall laid out the drawings and began explaining. They seemed impressed, and he could tell they thought many of the ideas were rather creative.

Nearly thirty minutes later, Marshall slouched back in his chair. "So, what do you think?" he asked, twirling a pencil between his fingers.

Boomer rubbed his bristly hair. "This is really swell and all, Marshall," he said. "But I'm not too sure we have the know-how to pull any of it off."

"I'm still thinkin' about that one," Marshall admitted. "But I've figured out a lot of it already." He turned to John and Fred. "I want you two to work on the soundtrack," he instructed. "Scary noises, the scarier the better. I don't care where you get them from; I don't care how you make them." He slid a diagram towards John. "This is our layout of what the whole thing will look like and how long it'll take to walk through. The soundtrack needs to sync up with where our guests will be during each portion of the tour."

John looked as if someone had just instructed him to move a large boulder to the top of a mountain.

"Can you handle that?" Marshall questioned. "I know you can do it," he added encouragingly. He then turned to Boomer. "You said you and your mom still have a couple horses, right?"

"Sure do," Boomer agreed.

"We need one," Marshall said flatly.

"Wh–what?" Boomer stammered.

"We need a horse. Can you ride?" Marshall continued.

Boomer jolted back, as if insulted. "Can I ride? Darn tootin' I can," he announced proudly.

"Just talk to your mom and do whatever you have to, but we need that horse," Marshall persisted.

"I'll try, Marshall," Boomer agreed, still appearing confused.

"Is there anything I can do?" Sam asked hopefully.

Marshall laughed. "I'm sure glad you asked," he said. "Jell-O."

"What?"

"Jell-O," Marshall repeated. "We need lots and lots of Jell-O. Ask your mom if she'll buy it for us, it's the least she could do after–" he couldn't bring himself to finish.

"What if she won't?" Sam questioned.

"We'll worry about that later," Marshall said dismissively. "My mom will help you make it."

"There's always room for Jell-O," John noted.

Sam glanced at John before returning her attention to Marshall. "What flavor?" she quizzed.

Marshall shook his head. "Doesn't matter, the weirder the better. Red, orange, green, yellow–go for it."

"Well, there ain't nothin' weirder than yellow Jell-O," Boomer chimed in before snatching up one of the sketches.

"Hey, I *like* yellow Jell-O," Fred declared.

Boomer leaned back in his chair and began studying the diagram intently. "There's still one thing I'm not gettin'," he said. "These drawings ain't anything like Fred's garage. There's no way we can do all this in there."

Marshall sighed; this was the part he had been dreading. "That brings us to the next step of our plan."

"Which is?" Sam asked, apprehensively.

Marshall and the others walked side by side up Radio Road. They passed by the park and stopped in front of the old, rusty, iron gate where they stood in silence, staring up at the rickety shutters and high-peaked roofs.

"It certainly looks haunted," Boomer commented.

"This guy scares me. Do you really want to do this?" Fred inquired.

"No," Marshall answered honestly. "But I will anyways."

He advanced slowly up the sidewalk leading to the front porch, as the others hesitantly followed. The only sound they could hear was their feet shuffling along the cement.

Marshall arrived at the end of the walk and stepped onto the porch while the others lingered behind. He reached up and rang the doorbell, sending an ominous tone echoing throughout the dwelling.

"Better add that to the soundtrack," Boomer whispered to John.

The door flung open and a familiar, bitter face glared down at them, as menacing and threatening as ever.

"What do you want?" Eustace growled.

Marshall's first instinct was to turn and run, but he stood firm. He struggled to find his voice, "Please, sir, we're students from your school, Goodson, and we were wondering–"

"Yeah, I thought I recognized you," Eustace interrupted. "Bunch of no good troublemakers! Botherin' me on a Sunday. It's not enough to make my life miserable five days a week, now you have to bother me on Sundays too!"

Marshall took a step back. "No, sir, we just–we," this wasn't going at all how Marshall had planned. "The big Halloween carnival is coming up, and we wondered if we could use your place for our haunted house?" he finally blurted out.

"You want to use my house?" Eustace said in a nearly polite tone.

"Yes, sir."

"Well, forget it!" Eustace barked.

Marshall felt dejected and slowly turned away.

"It was a good plan, Marshall," Boomer said quietly. "But you're just gonna have to admit that we can't beat them Benedict kids."

Eustace had turned, preparing to slam the door in their face, when he stopped abruptly. "Did you say Benedict?" he asked curiously.

"Yes, sir," Boomer spoke up. "There's this big contest with all the schools, to see who could raise the most money. The winner gets a trip to Wonderland!"

Eustace's mind seemed to drift far away as he began speaking. "I've given my whole life to Goodson," he said softly, lowering his head. "I went there as a boy, and I've worked there for nearly forty years. It was such a wonderful school," he whispered.

Gazing up, his eyes finally met Marshall's. "Until they built Benedict," he added bitterly. "Suddenly, no one cared for ol' Goodson. It was all about Benedict," he finished sadly. "Benedict, Benedict, Benedict." Then, his composure seemed to recover. "Why didn't you tell me that before, boy?" he said, stepping out onto the porch and slapping Marshall's shoulder. "If it's to beat a bunch of spoiled brats from Benedict, you bet I'll help."

Marshall smiled, fighting back his emotions. "Thanks, thanks a million, I can't—"

"On one condition," Eustace said, raising a finger in his customary, threatening fashion.

"Uh—sure, anything," Marshall agreed.

Eustace crossed his arms in defiance. "I get to go to Wonderland as a sponsor."

Marshall extended his right hand. "Agreed," he said.

Eustace accepted the handshake and grinned.

They arranged the details with Eustace regarding what times they could work in the evenings and other important issues. Walking back to the tree house, they were thoroughly excited.

"All right, but that just leaves us with one question," Boomer said. "How we gonna pull this stuff together?"

Marshall turned to John and smiled. "I think it's time I met your dad."

11.

The Bigger, The Better

The Beavers' Mechanic Shop didn't look much different in the daytime than it had at night. Only now, the doors were wide-open and Marshall could see the silhouette of a man hunched under the hood of a car.

The man must have heard the boys approaching because he straightened up and greeted them warmly, "Hey, boys."

Mr. Beavers was nothing like his son. He was tall and thin, with a thick, full beard and glasses. He wore a pair of beige coveralls, not unlike the pair the class had used to make their scarecrow. Large globs of fresh grease stained the front of the outfit and a name tag on the left-side read *Hi, my name is: Harry.*

"Mr. Beavers, we got us a problem," Boomer informed.

"Oh, really? What kind of problem?" Mr. Beavers inquired.

"Well, Marshall here can explain it better than I can. He seems to think you might be able to help us somehow." Boomer seemed to abruptly realize he had not yet introduced Marshall. "This here's Marshall Maddox, by the way, he just moved here this summer."

Mr. Beavers wiped the grease from his hands and reached out to shake Marshall's hand. "Yes, I believe your mom came in right before school started," Mr. Beavers remembered.

Marshall nodded as he shook Mr. Beavers' hand.

"So, what seems to be your dilemma?" Mr. Beavers questioned, focusing his attention on Marshall.

Marshall pulled the diagrams from his pocket and began showing them to Mr. Beavers. He tried desperately to explain his ideas, hoping Mr. Beavers could make them a reality. Marshall could see by Mr. Beavers' expression that his brain was already working on solutions to problems that hadn't even surfaced yet.

"But the thing is," Marshall said after several minutes, "those Benedict kids trashed everything and now we basically have a bunch of junk."

Mr. Beavers laughed. "Nothing's ever junk, Marshall," he advised. "You know that air conditioner in the tree house? Someone said they'd pay me to haul it off for them. They told me it was junk. I fixed it up and that thing's lasted through five hot summers."

Marshall smiled hopefully.

"So, do you think you can help us?" Boomer pleaded, cutting through the silence.

Mr. Beavers nodded. "I'll close up early every day this week if I have to, we'll finish it, somehow," he promised, returning his attention to his work.

The following day at school featured the next major obstacle, convincing Katy and the other girls that this new plan could work and be completed on time. At first, they weren't keen on the idea as he began explaining it. The girls kept shaking their heads or shrugging their shoulders.

Mrs. Green remained attentive and supportive as Marshall spoke. She was all for it. "We're the 6th grade class at the oldest school in town," she told her pupils. "We have to be represented. If we weren't, it just wouldn't be right."

"Besides," Boomer said, "do you just wanna lay down and die like a possum? That's what them Benedict kids want us to do."

The other boys thundered in agreement.

"Yeah!" one shouted.

"We can beat those snobs!" another yelled.

Jeremy sat in isolation, his arms crossed, without uttering a word. Marshall had politely omitted

Jeremy's role in the destruction of the haunted house when he relayed the story to Mrs. Green, but all of the kids knew the truth.

"There's just a few more things we need from the school," Marshall said, looking up at Mrs. Green. "I'd like to borrow a slide projector. If that's possible," he added, hoping he didn't sound too demanding.

"A slide projector?" Mrs. Green questioned.

"Yeah, the old kind, with the big plastic wheel on top that you put the slides in," Marshall explained.

Mrs. Green smiled broadly. "This looks like a job for the top hat!" she announced excitedly. She retrieved the sleek, black hat from the table, reached in and produced a name.

"Oh, Mrs. Green, do I have to?!" Boomer shouted before she even read the name.

Mrs. Green glanced down at the piece of paper. "John Beavers!"

Boomer and John both appeared stunned. John's name *never* came out of the hat.

"John," Mrs. Green said, "Could you go down to the library and ask Mrs. Wilson if we can borrow a slide projector?"

John nodded and rushed out the door.

Mrs. Green watched and as soon as the door had shut, she shifted her attention back to Marshall. "What else?"

Marshall turned to Katy. "I want to talk to your dad about something, if that's all right?'

Katy nodded. "Sure, but what could my dad—"

"I'll explain later," Marshall assured her.

Mrs. Green smiled curiously. "Is that all?"

Marshall smirked. "I need to borrow something from my mom's room," he told them, "but I'll ask her about that myself," he concluded dramatically.

Just then, John burst through the door, his face ghostly pale. *"Phantom Plopper!"* he yelled to a stunned room.

Katy dropped her head to the desk. "Not again, that is soooo gross," she moaned.

John shook his head rapidly. "No! I mean, they caught him!"

Everyone gasped at this stunning announcement.

"It was one of the 5th graders. Eustace caught him red-handed!" John exclaimed.

"Are you sure they were red?" Jeremy muttered.

Marshall glanced up at Mrs. Green and whispered, "I thought it was John."

Mrs. Green leaned forward towards Marshall. "We all thought it was John," she answered in a voice only Marshall could hear.

The week proceeded exactly according to Marshall's plan. Mr. Beavers had helped at Eustace's house each night. Fortunately, after conquering his arch-nemesis, the Phantom, Eustace had never seemed happier. He also appeared genuinely excited about the prospect of his home being used to frighten hundreds of children.

They had managed to salvage most of the trash bags and tarps and were now using them to cordon off sections of Eustace's property that he wished to keep private. Marshall had seized the bag with the large green B and tied it to a stake, which he hammered into the front yard, an emblem of defiance towards the Benedict kids.

On Wednesday evening, Marshall received a pleasant surprise when Jeremy arrived at Eustace's manor.

"Can I talk to you for a second?" Jeremy asked delicately.

"Sure, what's up?" Marshall replied, stepping away from the crowd.

"I just wanted to say I'm sorry," Jeremy apologized. "I'm sorry about everything. I'm sorry about wrecking the garage, I'm sorry I was so mean to Sam, and rude to you."

"Don't worry about it," Marshall responded awkwardly.

They strolled out onto the porch and Jeremy continued, "I guess I was just—jealous."

"Jealous? Of me?" Marshall inquired.

"Oh, come on, who wouldn't be jealous of you? From the moment you told everyone about surfing in Australia, you've been the coolest kid in school. You're the best athlete, you're smarter than anyone I've ever met, all the girls think you're cute, heck even your name is cool. *Marshall Maddox,*" he said with a flourish.

"Huh, I've never really thought of myself as cool," Marshall began, "and certainly not as being popu—girls think I'm cute?"

"Do you honestly think they were mean to Sam because she goes to a different school?" Jeremy asked. "They're jealous because she's your girl-friend," he explained.

"She's not my girlfriend," Marshall argued.

"Whatever you say, pal," Jeremy laughed. "But anyways, I just came over to say I was sorry an—and to ask if there was anything I could do to help?"

Marshall chuckled loudly. "All in good time. First, let me show you what we've done."

The two of them sauntered back inside and Marshall directed his attention to the landing overlooking the entryway. The twins were standing on the landing, struggling to untangle a knot.

"Hey, Mike!" Marshall called out. "Show Jeremy how Stanley works."

"Stanley?" Jeremy repeated.

"Yeah, he's been in my mom's closet since the first day of school," Marshall explained, pointing to a skeleton sitting on a bench.

Just then, the skeleton rose to its feet and began walking towards the stairs. It raised an arm and pointed at Jeremy.

"How's he doing that?" Jeremy gasped, staring in amazement.

Marshall gestured at Mike who was waving his

arms in time with the skeleton's movements. "It's like a marionette–a puppet," Marshall answered. "John's dad helped me rig it up. It's connected to fishing line we took from Fred's garage. We'll use black lights and the fishing line won't be visible at all. Our puppeteer," he pointed up at Mike, "will be dressed in black, so he won't be visible either."

"Cool!" Jeremy exclaimed.

"Look at this over here," Marshall indicated. "This is our Mad Scientist Laboratory. We borrowed this table from John's dad," he said, tapping on the table. "We took his tools out, and in these holes, will be our mad scientist's potions and concoctions. Sam's over at my house right now, she and my mom are making gallons and gallons of Jell-O which we'll use as a substitute for potions."

They stepped to the other side of the table. "And down here," Marshall continued, showing Jeremy the underside of the work bench, "we'll have a couple of people hidden, wearing those big rubber gloves that Mr. Beavers has. They'll reach up through the holes," Marshall mimicked the motion with his hand. "It should be a lot of fun."

"Who's the mad scientist?" Jeremy wondered aloud.

"Who else?" Marshall said, nodding towards John.

"Come look at this one," Marshall said proudly. "We figured this out together, Mr. Beavers and I, that is," he explained, noting the confusion on

Jeremy's face. "We bought this fog machine the night my parents took us to the Save-Mart, and it worked really well. Those Benedict kids roughed it up last Saturday, and we thought it was broken." Marshall flipped the machine on and copious amounts of fog began emitting from it. "John's dad opened it up and got it working again—not to mention, made it even quieter than before."

Jeremy nodded in approval.

"But that's just the start. Watch this!" Marshall motioned to John, who toggled a switch on the slide projector from the library. A ghostly image appeared in the fog. John slid the projector back and forth, and the image floated along with it.

"Awesome," Jeremy gasped.

"You see, the fog basically works as a screen, but since it's not solid, it gives the picture a ghostly effect. It's there, but it's not." Marshall stared at the projector for a moment. "We've had to cover as much of the lens as possible, because it was just producing too much light—" he started.

"What in the world is that a picture of?" Jeremy interrupted, his eyes squinting as they pursued the floating image.

"It's just John wearing a mask and that big, ugly green rain coat we found in Fred's garage."

Jeremy laughed. "What's next?"

"Over here, we have something I figured out myself," Marshall stated. "In the daylight, it doesn't look like much, but in total darkness, it definitely has the right effect."

They stepped into a hallway with nothing but four narrow mirrors on opposite walls and two candles.

"I don't get it," Jeremy admitted.

"Stand, right here," Marshall instructed, pointing to an X on the floor.

Jeremy stood on the spot. "Whoa, that's pretty wild."

"Since the mirrors are facing each other, when you stand right there, it gives the appearance of an endless row of candles in a hallway stretching into oblivion."

John, who had followed them into the hallway, studied Jeremy for a moment. "There are few things people fear more than the unknown," he said wisely.

"Exactly, John," Marshall agreed. "Now, through this door," he prompted.

Jeremy gripped the brass door handle and as soon as he did, a realistic-looking witch on a broom swept down a long flight of stairs. "Let me guess, Mr. Beavers again?" Jeremy questioned.

Marshall nodded. "It's a simple trick. He rigged it up on pulleys and ropes. Again, you won't be able to see those in the dark, just a witch flying down the stairs." Marshall gazed up at the ceiling as they ascended the steps. "And he promised Eustace he could put them up and take them down without leaving any evidence they were there–I hope," he added quietly.

They made it to the top of the stairway and Marshall motioned to the ceiling again. "Mr. Beavers' other contribution to the project is the sound system. He dismantled it from his shop and brought it over here. He set it up so everyone will be able to hear John and Fred's soundtrack."

The floor creaked beneath their feet as they stopped in front of a bedroom door. "In here," Marshall gestured, "Katy's dad is setting up some-thing, but he doesn't have it ready to go." He opened the door, allowing Jeremy to glimpse inside before they continued moving. "And in this room," he said, opening yet another door and walking through, "well, remind me to come back to that in a second."

They passed through the empty room and onto a balcony. It had been concealed by tarps so the yard wasn't visible, giving it the appearance of a small room with no roof. A park bench sat in one corner.

"Out here, we'll rebuild our scarecrow, wearing Mr. Beavers' old clothes. He'll sit with a bucket full of candy so kids can take a piece before they leave."

Jeremy nodded again and noted his approval as they stepped down a spiral staircase leading to the backyard.

"And back here," Marshall explained, "Boomer will have his horse. He'll be our headless horse-man."

"Headless horseman?" Jeremy inquired.

"Yet another one of John's dad's contributions. He rigged up this deal," Marshall picked up a device with a pump and narrow nozzle, "it supposed to be used for oil—or something like that." He pumped it several times, "But we'll put fake blood in there and squirt it out the top of Boomer's severed neck."

"But Boomer doesn't have a severed neck," Jeremy pointed out sensibly.

"Mr. Beavers had an old Halloween costume that's perfect for the occasion. It sits on Boomer's shoulders, so it looks like he doesn't have a head."

"I see," Jeremy replied.

At that moment, Boomer came charging into the yard. "Marshall, Marshall!" he shouted. "You'll never believe what I got!"

"What's that, Boomer?" Marshall chuckled.

"Come take a gander at this!" Boomer yelled, rushing around the side of the house.

Marshall and Jeremy followed to find Boomer's mom sitting in her minivan. Boomer opened the passenger side door, reached in and pulled out...

"The Baxter dummy?" Marshall laughed.

"Isn't it great?" Boomer said, holding up a head with shiny, black hair. Grinning ear to ear, Boomer held it by the hair like a tribal warrior who had just claimed the head as a prize. "I got the rest of it back here too," Boomer said enthusiastically.

"That's great, Boomer," Marshall encouraged.

Boomer stood beside them, still fixated on the head.

"But you still haven't answered my question," Jeremy began, "what can I do to help?"

Marshall clapped a hand on his friend's shoulder. "I'm glad you asked. You have the most important job of all."

12.

The Trick-or-Treaters

"Are you guys sure you want to do this?" Marshall pleaded. It was Friday afternoon, the day before Halloween. The boys were sitting around the tree house after school and Marshall was having second thoughts.

"Oh, come on, Marshall, you can't back out now," Jeremy chided. "I was the one who was against it in the first place, and now I'm all for it."

"Yeah, but–" Marshall started to protest.

"Besides," Boomer interrupted. "If we don't go trick-or-treatin', Fred'll probably never get the chance."

"All right," Marshall agreed reluctantly, "we'll do it for Fred."

Marshall exited the tree house and began treading the now well-worn path to his home. He glanced over and saw Sam strolling down Radio Road towards him.

"Hey, I was just coming to look for you," she stated.

"Yeah, we were just discussing our plans for tomorrow night," Marshall replied.

"You mean the haunted house?"

"No, trick-or-treating tomorrow, remember?" Marshall said with a lopsided smile.

"Oh yeah, Fred's never been has he?" Sam questioned. "So, why do you look so down?"

"Oh, I'm not really," Marshall answered honestly, "I was just trying to think of what I was going to wear for a costume."

Sam giggled. "It's the day before Halloween and you haven't even *thought* about a costume yet?"

Marshall pointed towards Eustace's house. "Well, we've been kind of busy," he said. "I don't have a clue what I should go as," he admitted.

"Hmmm, maybe I can help," Sam responded sweetly.

They continued up the sidewalk towards Marshall's house and stepped inside.

"Hi, Sam," Marshall's mom greeted brightly. "Have a good day at school?"

"It was all right," Sam returned.

"So, what are you two doing?" his mother asked.

"Marshall needs a Halloween costume and he doesn't know what to wear," Sam responded.

"Sounds like that might call for another trip to the Save-Mart," his mom suggested. "I need to pick up a few things, anyways. You two want to come along?"

Minutes later, they were on their way into the Save-Mart.

"I'll meet you guys in the Halloween Department," she said as they entered through the automatic sliding doors. "I'll go get my other things while you see what they've got."

As Marshall and Sam hurried away, they heard her add, "Nothing too scary!"

They found the Halloween department in shambles. Hundreds of kids had plowed through since Marshall and his friends had been there. Swaths of shelf space were now empty, or sparsely littered with ripped and broken items. The department offered precious little to choose from.

"Looks like you waited too long," Sam said, surveying the nearly barren aisles.

"Well, let's take a look anyways," Marshall responded. He plucked a red-caped costume from a rack full of duplicate outfits. "This one, maybe?"

"No," Sam said promptly. "There's a reason those are still here. How about this one?" she offered, holding up a brightly colored suit.

Marshall considered it for a moment. "I don't think so," he responded politely, "yellow's never been my color."

She shuffled through a couple more, deciding

against them on her own.

Marshall pulled a vampire's cape off the rack. "Dracula?" he asked.

Sam shook her head. "Please don't, Baxter goes as a vampire every year." She moved closer to him and grinned, "And the less you look like him, the better."

"Agreed," Marshall said, swiftly returning the cape to the rack.

Marshall and Sam continued sorting through the costumes.

"Indian?"

"No."

"Construction worker?"

"I don't think so."

"Biker? Soldier? Police Officer?"

"No, no, and no."

"Hmmm, well, you need to pick something," Sam said finally.

"This is hopeless," Marshall sighed.

"I'll admit, none of these seem to fit your personality," Sam agreed.

Just then, Marshall's mother arrived.

"Any luck?" she questioned hopefully.

"No," Marshall answered, dejected.

"Let's see, is there anywhere else in town that might have costumes?" Mrs. Maddox asked.

Sam shook her head. "Not really."

"Hmmm," his mother said, considering the dilemma. "This isn't over yet. Let's head home and take a look in the closets."

Marshall's mother paid for her purchases and they left, still pondering the problem. Upon returning home, the three of them traipsed upstairs and perused through several closets. With each door they opened, a few items were selected and laid on a bed. Before long, they had gathered enough clothing to costume five people.

Marshall slipped on an old cowboy hat that belonged to his father. Next, he tried on a tweed jacket with leather patches on the sleeve, which Marshall thought made him look too much like his dad. Finally, he sampled a judicious-looking robe his mother had worn at her college graduation.

Sam, still searching in the closet, reached to the back and pulled out a long, black coat. "What's this?" she asked.

Marshall's mother approached and stared at it curiously. "Oh, that's an outfit my husband had to wear to a very formal dinner at his last university."

Marshall tried the outfit on. As he stood, admiring himself in the mirror, he saw his father enter the room behind him.

"Picking out a costume, I surmise?" Dr. Maddox asked. He leaned over and kissed Mrs. Maddox on the cheek.

"Yeah," Marshall replied.

"You know, the Irish started our trick-or-treating tradition," the professor explained. "They called it guising and–"

"Not now, dear," Mrs. Maddox said with a chuckle.

"Well, anyways, it looks great," Dr. Maddox complimented.

"But it's just a suit," Marshall said, studying his reflection.

"It's just a suit now. But I've got just what you need to go with that," his father responded. He picked up a footstool at the end of the bed and placed it in the closet. Stepping on to it, he reached into the furthest depths of the top shelf and rummaged around. Seconds later, he pulled down a long, slender box. He returned from the closet and set the box gently on the bed.

Marshall watched as his dad removed the lid, revealing a short, black cane.

His father handed Marshall the cane before reaching into the box once more and withdrawing a pair of white gloves. Marshall slipped them on and examined himself in the mirror. The attire exuded a definite image that he found appealing.

Sam whistled approvingly. "I like it."

"But is it scary?" Marshall questioned.

"Well, I guess not," Sam confirmed.

"Actually," Dr. Maddox said, his voice sounding deep in thought, "if we could just find a top hat, you'd bear a striking resemblance to a famous serial killer from the late 19th Century."

"Top hat?" Marshall repeated, turning to his father. "I know where I can get one of those."

The following evening, Marshall donned the long, black coat and gloves. He picked up the sleek, black top hat from his desk and placed it firmly on his head. As 6:00 approached, he stepped downstairs to inform his parents that he was about to leave for trick-or-treating.

"Happy All Hallows' Eve!" his dad greeted.

Marshall smiled, just as the doorbell rang. He opened the door to find Sam dressed as a gypsy in a long flowing skirt and a loose-fitting, short-sleeve top. Her hair hung past her shoulders, as opposed to her customary ponytail, and various bracelets and other jewelry adorned her arms, fingers, and neck. A purple shawl draped around her shoulders.

Marshall smiled. "You look great," he said instinctively.

Sam blushed. "Thanks," she replied.

"Have a good time, you two," Dr. Maddox encouraged. "We'll see you at the carnival."

"And don't eat any candy until you bring it home first!" Marshall's mother warned as they shut the door behind them.

Marshall and Sam ventured down the street to the Beavers' home, where the others were already waiting on the porch. Marshall studied his friends' costumes while they gawked at his.

John was dressed in a loud, three-piece, pin-striped suit which featured a gold watch fob and a fedora hat. Marshall thought he looked very much like a mobster from a 1930s movie.

Jeremy, on the other hand, had gone a radically different direction. He wore what appeared to be an authentic baseball uniform, complete with cleats and a cap. "It used to be my dad's," he informed, "a long time ago."

Boomer had chosen a rather simple-looking pair of coveralls which looked suspiciously familiar. "I'm a mechanic!" Boomer shouted proudly. "Borrowed this from John's dad."

Marshall chuckled as Boomer twirled a socket wrench in his hand.

"Where's Fred?" Marshall asked.

"Oh, here he comes now," Boomer said, pointing his wrench.

Fred came strutting into the yard to a chorus of laughter. He wore a wide-brimmed hat, chaps, a leather vest, and a holster at his side which held what was obviously a toy gun. He even had a tin star pinned to his chest.

"These boots are a pain in the–" Fred started in English, but then slipped into Korean as he continued to complain.

"All right then, where do we start?" Sam asked.

"We'll just make our way up and down the street," Boomer suggested.

They approached the first house and rang the doorbell.

"Trick-or-treat!" they greeted.

"Oh, trick-or-treat!" Fred yelled belatedly.

They all received a handful of candy from a nice, elderly lady who complimented each of them on their costumes. As they walked away, Fred commented, "I still think it should be treat-or-trick."

Trick-or-treating on Radio Road was unlike anything Marshall had ever experienced. In his old town, most of the people left their porch lights off. Children were forced to attend business-sponsored parties or church activities if they hoped to receive candy.

Radio Road was different. Every family up and down the street had their porch light on. Various shades of orange decorated every window, with black cats and spiders on each door. The doorsteps were lined with gleaming jack o' lanterns and one house even had a colored light on their porch, which cast an eerie orange glow over the surroundings.

Each knock of the door resulted in a warm, welcoming smile. Several of the adults had even dressed up in costume for the night's revelry, and they all had buckets of candy for every kid who passed by.

After visiting most of the houses up and down Radio Road, the sound of a familiar voice sliced through the cool, crisp evening air.

"Hey, look who it is, Creature, a bunch of kids who think they're still in 2nd grade," Baxter sneered.

Marshall shivered as he turned and saw Baxter approaching, flanked on both sides by the oversized Creature and the short, squat Ricky. Just as Sam had predicted, Baxter was dressed in a black cape and fangs. His black hair had been slicked back to accompany his vampiric attire. He held one arm behind him, as if mimicking a proper gentleman.

Ricky was dressed just as Baxter, the cape not quite fitting his rotund frame. Creature, on the other hand, wore no costume at all, opting for a black T-shirt and jeans.

"Hey, Melville, what are you supposed to be?" Baxter asked Marshall. "You look like some sort of deranged butler or something." He didn't wait for a reply. "And Boomer there looks like he just got off work," he laughed, nudging Creature in the ribs.

John waved at Creature hopefully, but Creature did not return the gesture.

"And you," Baxter snickered, turning his attention to Fred and John, "I don't know either of you, but you're just plain weird."

"Well, they've got a big bag full of candy and you don't," Marshall defended.

"You shouldn't tempt us like that, Monty," Baxter cautioned, glancing down at the sack of treats in his sister's hand. "Besides, we'll get ours' later," he threatened. They laughed again and strutted away.

"Well, I got off pretty easy," Boomer said. "After all, I did just get off work."

Just then, Baxter's voice pierced the air again.

"Hey, losers!" he shouted, and Marshall caught sight of an egg as it smacked against Boomer's coveralls. Several more eggs sailed in their direction, one striking Jeremy on the neck, another splattering across Fred's shoulder. Fortunately, Baxter, Ricky, and Creature didn't have the greatest aim and most of the eggs shattered and splashed on the ground or whizzed wildly over their heads. They exhausted their supply rather quickly, and the three of them dashed off into the darkness.

As Jeremy wiped at his neck, the yellow yoke oozed through his fingers. "Ah, yuck."

Sam stepped forward and removed her shawl, offering it to him.

Jeremy stared at her, a puzzled expression on his face, before reaching out to accept the scarf. "Thanks," he said meekly.

"All right," Marshall finally said, "It's about time we get on over to the carnival. John and Boomer, you guys need to get changed."

Boomer waved a hand dismissively. "Just relax, Marshall, we've still got an hour before we need to change."

Marshall then turned to Jeremy, "And you probably ought to make sure everything's ready on your end," he continued.

"I'm on it," Jeremy answered, marching off towards Eustace's.

Marshall rubbed his forehead, taking in a deep breath of determination. "I just hope everyone else is ready for this."

"They will be," Sam encouraged. "You've got a great class and you've done a whale of a job getting them ready."

"Thanks," Marshall said, smiling. "I'll see you at the carnival."

13.

The Carnival

Marshall approached Radio Road Municipal Park in awe. Floodlights hummed overhead, providing illumination for the various classes that had set up booths throughout the park. Kids in Halloween costumes darted about and hundreds of adults were partaking in the festivities as well.

He knew his first priority was to check in at Eustace's and assure that everything was ready to go. As he drew near the front porch, Marshall encountered two of the least likely people he could imagine, Jamie and Jennifer.

"I thought you two weren't going to have anything to do with this," Marshall quipped.

"We felt bad that we gave you such a hard time

about it," Jamie started.

"And we wanted to do something to help make it up to you," Jennifer finished, kneeling to pick up a large roll of paper.

Together, Jamie and Jennifer began unrolling the parchment. The banner unfurled, slowly revealing the phrase:

THE GOODSON HOUSE OF FEAR

"That's fantastic!" Marshall exclaimed. "Let's hang it on the fence, that way people know where we are."

The girls rushed to mount the sign, and Marshall turned to CJ, who was preparing to take tickets. "Ready to go, CJ?"

"Ready as I'll ever be," CJ responded.

"Don't let any of them Benedict kids give you a hard time," Marshall added.

"I'll run 'em over if they do," CJ joked.

Marshall stepped into the house for one final look around. "You ready to go, Mike?" he called out across the room. Mike had changed into a white lab coat and a pair of goggles to man the first shift as the mad scientist.

Mike gave a thumbs up. Marshall turned to Katy who was readying herself to lead the first tour. "Everything good to go upstairs?" he questioned with uncertainty.

Katy nodded. "Who's taking this shift in the backyard?"

"Boomer's mom volunteered," Marshall confirmed.

"Excellent. Now, you go on out there and have some fun," Katy encouraged, "I got this."

"All right, I'll be back to replace you at eight o'clock," he assured her.

Marshall reluctantly left the house and joined the fray of the carnival, which was firing up all around him. Somewhere in the distance, the local high school marching band launched into their school fight song. The crowd buzzed, filling the air with laughter and frivolity. Everywhere Marshall looked, he could see adults and children alike engaging in whimsical celebration.

He weaved his way through the throng, struggling to find Jeremy and the others. He marched in the direction of the food vendors, thinking they might be there. But along the way, he heard his name called and turned to find Boomer and the rest, all laughing and out of breath.

"We was just over at the dunk tank and we got Sam's teacher soakin' wet!" Boomer announced proudly.

They fell in pace with Marshall and walked around, enjoying watching other people compete in various booth activities. Every once in a while, Boomer would stop and try his hand at throwing darts at balloons or seeing how many baskets he could sink in twenty seconds.

"You know," Marshall said after the third game Boomer had played, "if we want to win that contest, we shouldn't really be spending our tickets at other class's booths."

Boomer sighed. "The point of the carnival is to have fun, Marshall."

Several minutes later, they spotted Dr. Maddox. "Hey, Marshall, look what I won!" his dad shouted, waving a large stuffed kangaroo. Marshall recognized it as one of the prizes being given away by a local business.

"Hey, look at this! That cow's playin' bingo!" Boomer exclaimed.

They stopped and watched as a cow wandered around in a large square sectioned off into fifteen smaller squares.

"I don't get it," Boomer said, scratching his head.

They moved on before slowing up again at the cakewalk.

"Boy, if I knew which one of them cakes my Aunt Matilda made, I'd sure give it a shot," Boomer announced, eyeing the wonderful cakes and pies.

They made it to the back side of the carnival and spotted the Benedict Haunted House. They were using one of the homes along the north edge of the park and had an enormous setup in the backyard. From what Marshall could see and hear, it appeared that Benedict was utilizing many strobe lights and high quality sound effects.

"Has anyone been in there?" Marshall asked curiously.

"I haven't," Boomer said. "But my cousin went through it earlier, and he said that it was a regular ol' scare-fest. Just a bunch of people jumpin' out tryin' to scare ya."

Jeremy nodded in agreement. "I talked to another kid and it sounded like it was pretty much the same as our first one, only bigger."

Marshall frowned. "Well, hopefully people will give us some credit for originality."

They traveled the length of the carnival again, and when they arrived back at Eustace's, they were amazed at what met their eyes.

"A line?" Marshall said aloud. People were backed up, waiting to get into The Goodson House of Fear.

"You did good, Marshall," Boomer proclaimed, slapping him on the back.

Just then, Sam came running up, drenched from head to foot. "I just did my turn in the dunk tank," she complained. "I got dunked three times."

"Who'd wanna dunk you?" Boomer wondered.

"Take a guess," Jeremy said sarcastically.

"Baxter," Marshall returned flatly.

Sam nodded. "I've gotta go dry off," she explained.

"After you finish, you can help out here if you'd like," Marshall suggested as she ran off once more.

John, Boomer, and Jeremy went off to change

into their costumes. Marshall, however, was already wearing the perfect costume for his job. He cut his way to the front of the line and bumped into Katy, coming around the corner. She apparently had just finished leading another group through, and when she saw Marshall, she sighed with relief.

"I'm so glad you're here," she said. "I'm not sure I could bring myself to go upstairs one more time," she admitted.

"I was afraid it wouldn't turn out right," Marshall worried. He had been apprehensive about the upstairs for quite some time. Katy's dad had gotten his things in place at the last moment, and he wasn't sure how successful Jeremy and his mother had been with their part.

"No, it's not that," Katy said. "It's just–" she shook her head, "you'll see when you get up there."

CJ took tickets from the next group in line. "No more than six at a time, no more than six at a time!" he yelled in a voice that would have made any carnival barker proud. "Hand your tickets right here!"

Marshall opened the door, allowing the next group of visitors to enter. He stepped in behind them and closed the door, plunging them into darkness.

Forty-five minutes later, Marshall had led nine groups through the house and he was beginning to feel foolish saying the same words repeatedly. But he reminded himself, that with each group, it was the first time any of them had heard it. Sam had come over to help, and she had settled herself next to Mrs. Green and Brenda, who had replaced CJ taking tickets. They had quite a few, but of course, they had no way of knowing where they stood in terms of the contest. The crowd had died down and the carnival seemed to be winding its way to an end.

"Hey, Marvin, you runnin' this show?" asked a voice that Marshall knew all too well.

"Baxter," Marshall replied courteously.

"What are you doing here?" Sam snapped.

"I could ask you the same thing," Baxter returned, "seeing as how you don't even go to this loser school."

Sam prepared to push herself out of her seat, but Marshall waved her off.

"Anyways, Malachi," Baxter said, turning back to Marshall. "We just want to take the tour."

Marshall peered down at the wads of tickets in Creature and Ricky's hands. "Are you sure?" he prodded.

Baxter shrugged. "We've got it in the bag," he said offhandedly. "So, let's get this thing started."

Marshall nodded curtly and opened the front door. "After you, sirs," he said, adopting a deadpan voice, attempting to mimic an old scary TV show he used to watch.

Marshall followed them inside and closed the

door. Stanley, the walking skeleton, immediately greeted them. Even though he had seen it several times now, Marshall was still amazed at how good it looked under the black lights.

"*Greetings,*" Stanley said, waving an arm in front of him. Marshall did his best to avoid looking up at David manipulating the puppet strings above. "*We hope you enjoy your visit to our House of Fear, please stay with your guide, we would hate for anything to happen... to you.*"

"That's pretty cool," Ricky whispered.

Marshall took over at this point. "If you'll follow me, gentlemen, I'd like to show you the first stop during our tour. We call it Dr. Fear's Laboratory of Madness and Mayhem. Let us take a look and see what Dr. Fear is up to this evening."

Baxter chuffed. "Dr. Fear? More like Dr. Pepper," he said scathingly.

Creature and Ricky chuckled as Marshall led them across the room.

The strobe lights around the makeshift laboratory flickered on, and there stood John Beavers, wearing the white lab coat and goggles. His wild, curly hair perfectly completed the look of a mad scientist.

"Ahhh-ha-ha!" John shouted, at a pitch that Marshall had never heard from his friend before. "Let's see what is on the menu for today!"

John reached into one of the large glass vats of Jell-O and pulled out what appeared to be a brain.

He raised it up to his mouth and took a massive bite. Marshall knew the disgusting mass was merely a bunch of gummy worms compacted together, but it still grossed him out.

"Disgusting, man!" Creature shouted.

"And what else does the good doctor have for us?" Marshall asked calmly.

Right on cue, the kids hidden under Mr. Beavers' cabinet reached their hands through the holes, wearing rubber gloves and flinging copious amounts of Jell-O in the direction of Baxter, Creature, and Ricky.

"Ugh, what is that stuff?" Ricky moaned, backing away.

"Now, gentleman, if you'll follow me, I'll take you to our next stop."

They had just entered the area where the fog machine had been operating for quite some time. When they reached the appropriate marker, the image of John in the green raincoat began passing through the fog.

"What the heck is that?" Baxter yelped.

"There it is over there too!" Creature shouted as the apparition disappeared and reappeared across the room.

"Please, gentlemen," Marshall said, attempting to sound very bored. "We're losing valuable time. Right through this door, please."

Suddenly, the trash bags nearest to Baxter flew apart. He jumped more than a foot backwards, baffled by the silhouette of Eustace, which had just appeared.

"Who's that?" Baxter said stiffly.

Marshall raised his eyebrows. "Oh, that's Eustace. He lives here. Now, if you'll please follow me."

Baxter followed along. "He's not scary," he smirked, glancing over his shoulder.

Eustace crowed with laughter. "Are you kidding? I'm the scariest thing in this place. I'm an old man! Just think about it! Sixty years from now, you'll look exactly like me! Your back'll hurt every morning, your knees'll hurt every night! You'll keep your teeth in a jar by the bed!"

Baxter, Creature, and Ricky shuffled their way along behind Marshall, who turned and gave Eustace a subtle thumbs up.

"What's this?" Baxter questioned.

"This, gentlemen," Marshall explained, "is a hallway, you walk down it."

The three of them were standing directly in the center of the very short hallway, which featured mirrors and candles on either side, giving it the appearance of a long, dark corridor.

"I'm not walking through there, you can't tell where it goes," Creature commented.

Marshall shook his head. "But we have no choice, we must press on. We must not fear the unknown."

"I'm not afraid," Baxter replied. He took three

steps forward and ran headlong into the wall.

"Oh, I forgot to mention," Marshall said, trying not to laugh, "it's a very short hallway."

Creature and Ricky guffawed.

Marshall pointed to the door with the stairway behind it. "We'll actually be going through here, gentlemen, after you."

Creature opened the door and spotted the witch gliding straight at them. Ricky screamed like a little girl as a great witch's cackle echoed from the hidden speakers. Creature wrapped his arms around Ricky as the witch thudded to a stop, less than a foot from them.

"Ha," Baxter said contemptuously, scrutinizing his companions. "How can you be scared of something like that?"

Marshall and the others ascended the stairs. As they halted on the landing, faint sounds could already be heard emanating from the first room.

Marshall placed a hand on the doorknob. "I must warn you, gentlemen, before I open this, that behind this door, we'll find one of the greatest fears known to man," he cautioned.

He swung it open to reveal a horrified-looking patient strapped to a dentist's chair. Katy's father, wearing a white coat, approached the patient with a dentist drill in hand. The device whined, buzzing with the most ominous noise, intensified by the sound effects John and Fred had created. The patient kicked and wailed, flailing his legs in pretend pain as the dentist acted as if he were placing the drill against his teeth.

Creature clapped a hand over his mouth and backed away from the door.

"You afraid of dentists, Creature?" Baxter chastised.

Creature did not reply but nodded briskly.

Marshall closed the door. "We're approaching the end of our tour, but we do have one room left to view. If you'd kindly step this way," he said, pointing to the door at the end of the hall.

Baxter, Creature, and Ricky followed along as Marshall led them into a completely darkened room.

"Keep walking, gentlemen," Marshall urged.

"What are we supposed to be afraid of, the dark?" Baxter asked sarcastically.

Just then, what sounded like a bike horn squeaked in the darkness.

"What was that?" Baxter demanded, a note of panic in his voice. "And what's that smell?"

The room suddenly grew dim, with just enough light to see. A mass of clowns crowded the room; more than thirty in all. All sorts of clowns; happy clowns, sad clowns, and some that looked downright frightening. Marshall had been in here ten times now, and it still disturbed him. Jeremy and his mother had really come through.

The clowns didn't speak, they didn't laugh, they didn't cry, they didn't make funny balloon animals;

they simply stared. Baxter stood in stunned silence. All at once, the cloud of clowns crept in around Baxter and his companions...slowly, ever so slowly. The entrance to the room had been sealed off, so the only way out was the door leading to the balcony.

Baxter stumbled his way outside, with Creature trailing closely behind. Hunching over into deep, shaky breaths, he finally muttered, "I–I–can't stand clowns."

Marshall disregarded the statement as he led a distraught Ricky outside. "We have now completed our tour; please feel free to take some candy from Harry." Marshall motioned to the scarecrow sitting on the park bench. It was wearing beige coveralls with the familiar name tag which read *Hi my name is: Harry*.

Creature and Ricky were closer, so they cautiously inched their way towards the candy first. Noticing that nothing had happened to them, Baxter stepped over to the park bench and reached into the dish sitting in Harry's lap. Baxter shrieked as one of the rubber-gloved hands tightly gripped his arm. The scarecrow jumped off the bench and growled, waving both hands in the air as Baxter stumbled backwards, tripping over one of his cohorts.

Regaining his footing, Baxter spun around and rushed towards the spiral staircase, followed closely by Creature and Ricky.

Once they were clear of the landing, Mr. Beavers pulled off the space helmet and smiled. "That'll show 'em," he whispered.

Marshall laughed and ran down the stairs after them, just in time to witness the grand finale.

Boomer, as the headless horseman, reared his mount back on its hind legs as the full moon shined in the sky behind him. The horse's front end came down and the animal began galloping towards the three boys, crimson liquid spurting from the top of the horseman's neck. Boomer reached into a saddlebag and yanked out the head of the Baxter dummy, raising it up by the hair, before swinging it underhand and lobbing it at Baxter's feet.

Baxter lost all control. He charged through the exit and back onto the street. "Those Goodson kids are nuts!" he shouted.

"Way to go, Boomer!" Marshall cheered. "That was awesome!"

"Did you see the way that turkey ran?" Boomer laughed, leaning forward in the saddle.

Baxter and his gang were the last customers for the night, and Marshall was glad of it. He met Sam in front of the house, and together, along with Boomer, John, Jeremy, and Katy, they walked towards the park as Mr. Daniels prepared to announce the winner of the contest.

They found Fred halfway there, who instantly began complaining about how boring his class's booth had been.

"This sure has been a great carnival," Boomer said.

Almost everyone had gathered around the platform where Mr. Daniels was approaching the microphone.

"Thank you, everyone!" Mr. Daniels announced. "Thank you for coming out tonight, and thank you for making the first annual Radio Road Halloween Carnival a smashing success!"

The crowd cheered enthusiastically.

"Now, I know what all of you have been waiting for, and I know you need to get on home, so without further ado, we will announce the winner of the big class trip to Wonderland!"

The crowd roared again, this time with even more energy.

"It was an extremely close contest and we want to thank all the classes who participated, but in the end, there can only be one winner," Mr. Daniels continued. He reached into the envelope which held the results. "And the winner is...wow," Mr. Daniels said, "this *was* close." After regaining his composure, Mr. Daniels went on, "And the winner is–by only *two* tickets–Mrs. Green's 6th grade class from Goodson Intermediate!"

A swell of emotions overwhelmed Marshall, he couldn't believe his ears. He stood, stunned, unable to comprehend that they had actually won. Sam rushed in and gave him a giant hug, lifting him several inches from the ground. The boys in his class funneled through the crowd, slapping him on the back and offering up high-fives.

Katy embraced Jeremy, who still wore his face-paint and brightly-colored costume. Even Eustace partook in the jubilation. Marshall noticed a tear in the old man's eye as he thrust his arms skyward, nearly knocking over one of the celebrating clowns.

From across the park, Marshall caught a glimpse of Baxter, Creature, and Ricky sulking away, shaking their heads in disgust.

"Well, you did it, Marshall," Jeremy said, wrapping an arm around his shoulder.

Marshall shook his head and beamed, "No, *we* did it," he corrected.

As the gathering began to break up, Sam returned to Marshall's side. "Tonight was a lot of fun," she smiled, suddenly taking his hand in hers. "But I've got to go. Would you like to walk with me."

"Sure," Marshall replied, "Just give me one second."

He turned and walked back to Jeremy. "Uh, I gotta go," Marshall stammered.

"What?" Jeremy asked.

Marshall shook his head and shrugged. "Maybe she is my girlfriend."

Jeremy laughed, smiling broadly through his painted-on frown. "I told you so."

Fifteen minutes later, Marshall arrived home

with the top hat in hand. It had been an incredible day, and he leaned back against the living room door, still attempting to absorb it all. He trudged upstairs and removed his costume, draping it over a chair. He plopped down next to the window, twirling the top hat between his fingertips as he gazed affectionately in the direction of Goodson School.

Somewhere up above, a cloud passed and the windows of Mrs. Green's 6th grade classroom suddenly basked beneath the light of a full moon. Marshall smiled. He had just experienced the best Halloween ever, and it was all because life had led him to Radio Road.

Jake Henderson was born and raised in Enid, OK, where he lived until attending college.

He attended Southwestern Oklahoma State University, in Weatherford, OK, where he earned a BA in History Education. He also has a Master's Degree in History Education from SWOSU, which he earned in 2004.

He has taught US History, World History, AP Government, Geography, Oklahoma History, and Psychology at the High School level for more than ten years, and he currently lives and teaches in Woodward, OK.